The Way Back
Rosalie White

Published by

MELROSE BOOKS

An Imprint of Melrose Press Limited
St Thomas Place, Ely
Cambridgeshire
CB7 4GG, UK
www.melrosebooks.com

FIRST EDITION

Copyright © Rosalie White 2011

The Author asserts her moral right to
be identified as the author of this work

Cover designed by Hannah Belcher

ISBN 978 1 907040 81 8

Printed and bound in Great Britain by:
CLE Digital Solutions. St Ives, Cambridgeshire

FSC
Mixed Sources
Product group from well-managed
forests and other controlled sources

Cert no. TT-COC-003115
www.fsc.org
© 1996 Forest Stewardship Council

This is dedicated to all those young people growing up in a computerised, mechanical, packaged world.

If there was a FINAL SHUTDOWN, would they know how to find THE WAY BACK?

CHAPTER 1

The first flakes of the January snow crept over the tall buildings of the city, which were outlined stark and ugly in the clean, still air. At ten o'clock on a January morning Glasgow was strangely quiet, hushed. Smoke could be seen rising at intervals here and there; not from any of the buildings, but from bonfires on the ground.

Near the centre of the city, one family was beginning to stir. Most mornings there was no hurry, no anxiety about getting up and out. Everyone knew by now that bed was the best place to be, to conserve heat and energy. For the McBrides, this morning was different.

It was Andy's turn to stoke the district bonfire, and collect wood to keep it burning through the morning. Ever since the 'Final Shutdown', the Men's Committee had taken turns to carry out and organise this task. The fires were vital for warmth, for water for tea and hot bottles for the beds, for simple cooking, and as a focus for such community life as was left.

It had been easier in summer. Just after the shutdown happened there had been an air of excitement, of adventure. Something new and strange had challenged the usual, dull routine. Now, stoking the fire in the cold had become part of the routine too.

Andy stumbled from the bed, wrapping the blankets closely round Sheena and the still-drowsy children. He, Sheena, Helen and wee Jim all shared the bed. There was another bedroom in the flat but, with the onset of the cold weather, they needed all the heat they could get.

Andy pulled his jersey on over his T-shirt. He was a big man, but gone to seed after years of unemployment, beer drinking and bad diet. His belly bulged slackly over his trousers. His tattooed arms were white and flabby. Despite his unsavoury appearance, he was known locally as a quiet, decent, big fellow.

He looked down from his eighth floor at the smoky fire below, and pondered on the problem of wood collection for the day. Most of the park benches had gone, and all the trees from roundabout had long since disappeared to fuel the fires. He knew he would have to go further afield, maybe to outskirts; and he'd have to borrow a handcart to haul the wood back.

He collected the blackened kettles and saucepans, and filled them to take down to heat for the breakfast cups of tea, and the household washing. Sheena had given up trying to clean them now, and the wood smoke had them black and sooty beyond recovery.

Big John Mulloy was coming up the stair as Andy was going down. With a family of six up on the twelfth floor, John did not make the journey more than was absolutely necessary, since the Final Shutdown had done for the lifts.

Andy exchanged the time of day with him. John had done the early stint on the bonfire, getting it going, and keeping an eye out for prowlers from other districts stealing wood.

Now he was off for a long lie, and to send his noisy brood down for the day. He could not stand them underfoot all the time.

They commiserated over the onset of the snow, and mouthed their general fed-upness over the total situation. It was old ground now, nothing new left to say. Andy's usual crack about how fit John was getting with all the stair climbing died on his lips, for the man was gaunt and haggard, his lips blue. No joke up there with that fretful wife and all those kids, reflected Andy as he clattered on down, with his pots and kettles.

Outside in the searing air, the wind was blowing the black smoke in choking blasts, and ashes and bits of plastic and polystyrene from the edge of the bonfire were drifting about the square.

There was enough wood to do for a while, he thought with relief, as he surveyed an old door propped up against the wall. He'd break up a bit and chuck it on. That would give him time for breakfast and a trip to the corner shop to see what food could be purchased for the day. He worried about the latter. The dole was still coming, but another cut was rumoured – that would be the third. Still, there were no heat bills any more, no TV rental or licence to pay, and it was months since the rent had been collected. The rubbish was not much of a problem yet: it all went on the fires. In fact, it was many a long day since the streets had been so clean.

There was a black pot already on the fire, he noted. At first, at this time, there would have been a dozen pots, and a queue of people waiting, all laughing and talking in the sunshine, brought together by the initial drama and excitement of the crisis. Now, people with contacts in the country, or a chance to move to the fringes of the city, had gone, and those left were for the most part too cold and too apathetic to bother to come down until much later in the day.

He recognised the black pot. It belonged to the young Logans, Dougie and Margaret, who stayed on the floor above him. He bent to poke the fire under it, just as Margaret appeared from the doorway, clutching a rug around her for warmth. Andy glanced up at her, taking in the red eyes with the great purple shadows under them, and the pale tear-streaked face. His eyes travelled to the yellowing bruises on her arms. Things didn't seem to be going too well up there, he thought. Dougie had always been a tough customer, and Margaret had a fiery temper to go with her red hair and green eyes.

"Why don't ye go in to see Sheena?" ventured Andy. "It'll be a while before I get back up." Andy was never one to interfere with his neighbours' affairs, but his concern overcame his usual reticence.

"Ay, maybe I will," said Margaret, brightening. "Anyway, I see you've company coming that I can well do without."

Andy turned to look, and grinned. The 'Wierdies' were up and about. The Wierdies were not so much a gang as a collection of aimless, drifting, homeless kids. They shacked out in the theatre hall, sleeping at night on the benches and prancing about the stage, singing, dancing, shouting, enjoying their self-made limelight. They injected their veins with dye – the newest craze – turning their skin into a kaleidoscope of colour. They cut carefully shaped holes in their clothes so that this adornment showed through to the greatest effect. They were harmless, ineffective, good-natured. The Men's Committee looked in at times to see what they were doing, and made them shift their rubbish to the fire.

Andy liked going over to the theatre. Sheena had had a cleaning job there once, and had a great time. At the beginning of the shutdown the actors put on free shows and, cut off from the nightly dope of TV, everybody went.

The Wierdies clustered around the fire, crouching to get warm, scratching, giggling, but keeping a wary watch over their shoulders to see if the 'Wolverines' were about.

They were much less harmless – ex-Borstal boys with their own code, leaders and rules. They were tough, secretive, private. They lived in the abandoned buses which littered the streets. There they assessed all the comings and goings in the district, and used them to their advantage.

"If you guys are going to be here a while," said Andy, "you can keep the fire stoked. I'm away up for my breakfast."

Sheena was washing the children in the tepid water from the night's hot-water bottles, and was full of chat about Margaret's visit.

"Do you think you should speak to the Men's Committee about her bruises?" she queried, as they sipped their tea, warming their hands round the cups.

"I don't know," muttered Andy uneasily. "That's not the kind of business they deal with. It's not our affair either." He looked suspiciously at Sheena.

"I dinna like it," said Sheena. "Not with another bairn on the way. Well, we'll leave it for now."

She paused. "If you're going out to look for wood, maybe you could go up by the allotments and see if Sandy Wilson can spare ye a cabbage."

Andy was pleased. He always enjoyed a crack with Sandy and it would put in the morning. Sandy lived on the ground floor. He was a tight, wee man, brown and wizened like a raisin; a great man for the outdoor life. For years, every weekend he was off on his bike at dawn with his cycling club, up Loch Lomond, or down the Clyde coast. He was a great chat – about the old days, the characters he met on his travels, the drum-ups, and the singsongs by the roadside. Come to think of it, mused Andy as he trudged through the silent empty streets, he hadn't seen Sandy about for a while. He was always at his allotment.

He saw Sandy from afar, sitting on the bench outside his wooden shed, his little brazier giving off a great smell of wood smoke; and a good red glow too, Andy noted as he drew nearer.

"Man, it's grand doon here," he shouted. "Hoo come I've no seen you about this while?"

Sandy, wasting no words, gesticulated towards the hut, opening the door. Andy looked in. Trust Sandy to make the best of it. The hut was neat and organised, with a camp bed along one side. A deck chair, a small wooden chair and a folding table took up the floor space. There were shelves with pots and kettles and tins, candles, maps and books – for Sandy was a great reader, and was known to say often that the greatest man in his reckoning was Andrew Carnegie.

"I have it all here," he beamed at Andy. "Whit more do I want at my age? A roof, a fire at the door, my food growing, a dander up to the library. At least it's still open. They haven't thought of burning the books yet." He turned to Andy. "Now you, you have the family to think of. Hoo are things over there? Can you hold out over the winter?"

The two men humped together companionably over the brazier, and Andy told him the latest about the Men's Committee, the doings of the Wierdies and the Wolverines, of his suspicions about the relationship of Margaret and Dougie, and his ever-present worry about finding food and fuel.

Left alone, Sheena poured another cup of tea and sat turning the events over and over in her mind. The Mulloy child; the dogs; the times she had watched the rats scuttle among the buildings, getting bolder and closer each day. She shivered. What had they to lose anyway? If they could find some place to be together, and give the bairns some kind of chance at life, it would be enough. Some day, surely this would all be over. For the first time in her life, she was forced to contemplate a dramatic change in her way of life, and make a decision she could barely comprehend. Life had never been easy, but it had followed the accepted pattern of the place she grew up in, and the people she knew. School, work if you were lucky, early marriage, the council flat, kids, managing n the dole – these were the almost inevitable steps for most. This was the framework of existence she accepted and under-od. It had already been severely jolted by the Final Shutdown. ne had told her how to survive, to keep warm and cook and after children – in a high-rise flat – but at least here the place e people were familiar. She got up, as Andy had, and looked t the desolation of the square; the drab, derelict buildings; little blue cap still lying in the mud.

n Andy came back she had decided. She was unsure and t his idea of going north held out a glimmer of hope, a something. Here there was no hope at all – a country vernment, money, or foreseeable future.

"They say," said Sandy slowly, "that things are better in the north: more wood, the chance of rabbits and hares, and maybe a deer. They're bringing down peat to keep the hospital fires going. A fellow told me there's plenty more where that came from, when they get properly to work on it. There's plenty empty houses too – up there," he added reflectively.

"God save us," said Andy. "That would be rough again, livin' like that."

His only forays from Glasgow had been on trips with 'the boys' to Blackpool, and a couple of visits with the family to Butlins at Ayr. The dance halls and a bevy-up were his idea of a good weekend: no humping off with a rucksack as big as a house to sleep on a mountain, or pushing a bike through thick and thin, like wee Sandy.

On the trip home he pondered uneasily over his conversation. No, no, things would get better. They were more organised since the day of the final cut-off. Nobody believed it really would happen. There had been cut-offs before and they'd managed, always knowing that if they held on, the power would come back. But now it was six months, and the wood supply within reach was almost gone. There was looting and vandalising of the big shops in Argyll, and Sauchiehall, and Buchanan Streets in the search for anything that would burn, and the worst of the winter still to come.

There was no direction from 'above'. Glasgow had been declared one of the 'unmanageable' areas, and its citizens left to their own devices. The police were still in evidence but turned a blind eye, for the most part, to anything short of murder.

The enthusiasm of the Men's Committee was on the wane too. It had been all 'go' at first, like a big street party all the time, with everybody helping, doing jobs for the elderly, and games and lemonade for the young. Now, all the energy and effort left was focused on the communal fires; keeping the rota going for the gathering, guarding, chopping. That was what mattered.

Agonising, Andy turned the corner, which brought him into the draughty square formed by the blocks of the housing scheme. Suddenly he was plunged into a scene of frenzied rushing and shouting, then wild screams and the excited barking of dogs.

A fight, thought Andy. Were the Wierdies and the Wolverines at it again? Were his kids out?

He began to run towards the thick of the crowd, into the stinging smoke, his eyes scouring the faces, panting anxiously, shoving past people, until he pulled up rigid with shock and disbelief at what he saw.

The dogs were pulling, tearing, gnashing at a little red, sodden bundle which was being dragged this way and that through the black puddles and the yellow slush. The dogs were so maddened with hunger, grown wild with neglect, and excited with the taste of blood, that no one could get near them. People were ineffectively throwing stones and lashing at them with belts and sticks.

Andy saw the little blue cap sodden in the mud, and caught a glimpse of red hair. It was the youngest Mulloy child.

"Jesus," he gasped. "Oh, God, stop them!" He lumbered forward, grabbing at the charred wood, the kettles, anything he could clutch to throw. The air was hoarse with inarticulate cries of frenzy and despair.

Suddenly the crowd parted. The Wolverines had arrived, knives flashing, boots and chains thrashing, thuds; snarls and screams from the dogs. This was their scene, their action. They were the men of the hour, in for the kill.

Then there was a great silence. The crowd parted as Mulloy came through. Ashen faced, he picked up and turned over the mangled, dripping little body. Three dogs lay dead; others howled and snarled on the horizon, cowed for the moment.

People began to make soft, incoherent noises of sympathy, and arms reached out.

Andy retched violently and turned away, stumbling and gasping his way up the stair. Sheena, who had seen all from th window, met him on the landing, trembling with shock. T clung to each other, shaking. Andy thumped the doorjamb agonised frenzy.

"That's it," he shouted hoarsely. "We're getting ou enough. It'll be our kids next – if no the dogs, the rat

"Sit down, sit down," said Sheena. "There's w tea."

They drank in silence, hands trembling still ing back to their numbed bodies and minds.

"Did you know what ye were saying, A landing – about getting out of here? Whe

"Sandy was telling me it's better u peat and a chance of food," he mutte

"Where up north? How would

"We'd have to walk," he ver

"Walk!" Sheena was outra only walking you've ever d Say no more!" She gave a

Andy walked over Wolverines were hel a sheet and load it stayed down there to

"They say," said Sandy slowly, "that things are better in the north: more wood, the chance of rabbits and hares, and maybe a deer. They're bringing down peat to keep the hospital fires going. A fellow told me there's plenty more where that came from, when they get properly to work on it. There's plenty empty houses too – up there," he added reflectively.

"God save us," said Andy. "That would be rough again, livin' like that."

His only forays from Glasgow had been on trips with 'the boys' to Blackpool, and a couple of visits with the family to Butlins at Ayr. The dance halls and a bevy-up were his idea of a good weekend: no humping off with a rucksack as big as a house to sleep on a mountain, or pushing a bike through thick and thin, like wee Sandy.

On the trip home he pondered uneasily over his conversation. No, no, things would get better. They were more organised since the day of the final cut-off. Nobody believed it really would happen. There had been cut-offs before and they'd managed, always knowing that if they held on, the power would come back. But now it was six months, and the wood supply within reach was almost gone. There was looting and vandalising of the big shops in Argyll, and Sauchiehall, and Buchanan Streets in the search for anything that would burn, and the worst of the winter still to come.

There was no direction from 'above'. Glasgow had been declared one of the 'unmanageable' areas, and its citizens left to their own devices. The police were still in evidence but turned a blind eye, for the most part, to anything short of murder.

The enthusiasm of the Men's Committee was on the wane too. It had been all 'go' at first, like a big street party all the time, with everybody helping, doing jobs for the elderly, and games and lemonade for the young. Now, all the energy and effort left was focused on the communal fires; keeping the rota going for the gathering, guarding, chopping. That was what mattered.

Agonising, Andy turned the corner, which brought him into the draughty square formed by the blocks of the housing scheme. Suddenly he was plunged into a scene of frenzied rushing and shouting, then wild screams and the excited barking of dogs.

A fight, thought Andy. Were the Wierdies and the Wolverines at it again? Were his kids out?

He began to run towards the thick of the crowd, into the stinging smoke, his eyes scouring the faces, panting anxiously, shoving past people, until he pulled up rigid with shock and disbelief at what he saw.

The dogs were pulling, tearing, gnashing at a little red, sodden bundle which was being dragged this way and that through the black puddles and the yellow slush. The dogs were so maddened with hunger, grown wild with neglect, and excited with the taste of blood, that no one could get near them. People were ineffectively throwing stones and lashing at them with belts and sticks.

Andy saw the little blue cap sodden in the mud, and caught a glimpse of red hair. It was the youngest Mulloy child.

"Jesus," he gasped. "Oh, God, stop them!" He lumbered forward, grabbing at the charred wood, the kettles, anything he could clutch to throw. The air was hoarse with inarticulate cries of frenzy and despair.

Suddenly the crowd parted. The Wolverines had arrived, knives flashing, boots and chains thrashing, thuds; snarls and screams from the dogs. This was their scene, their action. They were the men of the hour, in for the kill.

Then there was a great silence. The crowd parted as Mulloy came through. Ashen faced, he picked up and turned over the mangled, dripping little body. Three dogs lay dead; others howled and snarled on the horizon, cowed for the moment.

People began to make soft, incoherent noises of sympathy, and arms reached out.

Andy retched violently and turned away, stumbling and gasping his way up the stair. Sheena, who had seen all from the window, met him on the landing, trembling with shock. They clung to each other, shaking. Andy thumped the doorjamb in an agonised frenzy.

"That's it," he shouted hoarsely. "We're getting out. I've had enough. It'll be our kids next – if no the dogs, the rats."

"Sit down, sit down," said Sheena. "There's water boiled for tea."

They drank in silence, hands trembling still, but warmth filtering back to their numbed bodies and minds.

"Did you know what ye were saying, Andy – out there on the landing – about getting out of here? Where would we go?"

"Sandy was telling me it's better up north – wood to burn and peat and a chance of food," he muttered.

"Where up north? How would we get there?"

"We'd have to walk," he ventured, having thought no further.

"Walk!" Sheena was outraged at the idea. "Can ye see us? The only walking you've ever done is down the Barras on a Sunday. Say no more!" She gave a sarcastic laugh.

Andy walked over to the window and stared down. The Wolverines were helping Mulloy to wrap the small body in a sheet and load it onto the handcart. Christ! He should have stayed down there to help. He grabbed his cap and was off.

Left alone, Sheena poured another cup of tea and sat turning the events over and over in her mind. The Mulloy child; the dogs; the times she had watched the rats scuttle among the buildings, getting bolder and closer each day. She shivered. What had they to lose anyway? If they could find some place to be together, and give the bairns some kind of chance at life, it would be enough. Some day, surely this would all be over. For the first time in her life, she was forced to contemplate a dramatic change in her way of life, and make a decision she could barely comprehend. Life had never been easy, but it had followed the accepted pattern of the place she grew up in, and the people she knew. School, work if you were lucky, early marriage, the council flat, kids, managing on the dole – these were the almost inevitable steps for most.

This was the framework of existence she accepted and understood. It had already been severely jolted by the Final Shutdown. No one had told her how to survive, to keep warm and cook and look after children – in a high-rise flat – but at least here the place and the people were familiar. She got up, as Andy had, and looked down at the desolation of the square; the drab, derelict buildings; and the little blue cap still lying in the mud.

When Andy came back she had decided. She was unsure and afraid, but his idea of going north held out a glimmer of hope, a promise of something. Here there was no hope at all – a country without a government, money, or foreseeable future.

CHAPTER 2

For a month they planned and made preparations. There was a new excitement, which gave a purpose for each day and a zest in carrying it out. There were trips to wee Sandy for information and advice; there were lists to be made, with his help; a whole new vocabulary of the outdoors to be comprehended; and rucksacks, sleeping bags, transport and tents to be discussed.

They had no plan about where to go. Sheena remembered her grannie, who came from Skye in the old days, and who related half-remembered tales of fishing and ceilidhs, and wedding parties that lasted for days. Her own excursions beyond Glasgow were even more limited than Andy's. With a da on the dole, and herself one of six kids, these circumstances did not allow for more than a few day trips to the Clyde coast, or a school outing to Edinburgh on the bus. Some of Andy's friends went youth hostelling and camping with the Boys Brigade, but Andy and Sheena had never been induced to see pleasure or interest in such pursuits. To them, up north was associated with discomfort and isolation – not much good for a laugh. Now it had become the promise of survival.

Andy did a deal with Mick, the leader of the Wolverines: the doors of his flat, and any furniture that would burn when they'd gone, in exchange for the warm anoraks, tent, sleeping bags and

primus – items that the Wolverines would know how to procure.
Thus far, Sandy's advice was followed, but on other matters
Andy and Sheena had ideas of their own. Never accustomed to
much communication, they now talked like excited children. A
handcart, they decided, was what was needed. Helen and Jim, at
seven and five, were too wee to walk far, and indeed never walked
anywhere but to the shops, and, in summer, to the nearest park.
They could put a mattress on the cart, for sleeping on the ground
was something they could not contemplate. Sandy was politely
dubious about this arrangement, and the Wolverines incredulous
and vastly entertained, but Sheena was adamant. Where the kids
were concerned she was on her own ground.

Two of the Wolverines, with the authority of the adventure
training they had been forced to undertake in remand homes and
centres, deputed themselves to speak to Andy.

"Ye cannae pull a handcart on they roads. Ye'll no last a day."

But Sheena held firm. The Wolverines, confronted not by
authority, but with utter helplessness and innocence, were at a loss
and became almost friendly.

To them, big slack Andy and Sheena pulling a handcart up
north was a new and highly amusing source of diversion.

"See you, Sheena. Will you wear your curlers, and they big,
red high heels?"

"It's the fags that'll keep you going, Andy – a puff a push."

"I'd like to see youse layabouts dey it," growled Andy
good-naturedly.

"Could dey it wi our hands tied behind our backs."

"Show us," said Andy, and somehow in the exchange of jibes
and insults, it was arranged that on the day of departure they were
to have an escort of Wolverines pulling the handcart to outskirts

of the city. The volunteers emerged from the pack as individuals: Big Mick; the hard, scar-faced Fergie; sullen Jemmy; and Noddy, the glue sniffer.

The Mulloys, aroused from their grief and apathy, proffered what help they could. Mulloy, who had driven a lorry in more prosperous days, brought them down a piece of tarpaulin to cover the cart – a necessity which had not occurred to Andy and Sheena. Dougie and Margaret watched the preparations anxiously and enviously, Margaret's burgeoning belly proclaiming her inability to do anything other than watch and wait.

Indeed the proposed trip of the McBrides provided a surge of interest and a talking point among the neighbours, which saw them all through the drear cold of the winter months.

CHAPTER 3

The onset of spring announced itself, not with any great outburst of green leaves and singing birds, but by a gradual increase of the thin sunlight, which gave a glimmer of warmth to the dark concrete of the buildings. It filtered through the grimy windows of the McBrides' flat, bringing some measure of cheer to the icy dark rooms, making Sheena's carefully arranged plastic roses on the sill look almost warm and alive.

Andy and Sheena knew the time had come to go, and faced with the reality of it all, they looked fearfully at each other, at their box-like rooms, at the washing machine, the TV, the fridge, the electric fire, all of which had hitherto been the expression of their strivings and ambitions. All useless now, but familiar. All they had, and all they knew.

On the morning of the great departure, the street was up and alive. For the neighbours it was again a happening, a gala. Sheena and Andy had assumed a new importance. They and their children were the centre of advice and attention. Mrs Mulloy put in a rare appearance to make tea for all round the fire. Wee Sandy came down on his bike, with an axe and a map to add to the box of useful articles he had already gathered. He cast a worried look at the cart. "Well, I suppose it will help youse on your way," he

proffered mildly. The Wierdies joked with the children, and Mr
Mulloy fussed over the tarpaulin, adjusting and readjusting the
load to make a place for the children to sit among the cardboard
boxes of food, and the tent, and the big canvas sack Sandy had
given for their clothes.

Then the Wolverines arrived. Leaders of the pack, but leaders
nonetheless; and with an air of authority and command they took
over the cart, hoisting the children on top of the load.

Sheena and Andy shook hands solemnly all round. Andy
swung the unaccustomed rucksack uneasily onto his shoulders.
Sheena picked up her carrier bag full of sandwiches, odds and
ends and drinks for the road, and they moved forward. They were
away.

A cheer from the neighbours was the last thing they heard as
they turned the corner. A couple of the younger Wierdies tagged
behind, curious, and wanting to be part of the spectacle.

Suddenly Sheena took Andy's hand – a gesture she had rarely
made since their courting days. "I feel kinda daft," she said. "It's
like a sorta dream."

"Aye," said Andy heavily. "Well, we'll just have to see how it
goes." He adjusted the rucksack. Suddenly, he felt very responsi-
ble for his little family.

Towards the late afternoon they were nearing the outskirts of
the city. The Wolverines, still determined to show their mettle,
pulled and pushed energetically at the cart, the two in front taking
turns with the two behind. The kids, worn out by the jolting and
the excitement of the day, had fallen asleep. Andy and Sheena
lagged wearily behind. The feeling of the daftness of it all was
gone. The city they had passed through, their city, had scarcely
yielded them a parting glance. Scenes like these were all too

familiar nowadays. Everywhere, houses were boarded up, and the little groups of people outside shops were too intent on the business of procuring the necessities of life, to register either surprise or amusement. No, their feelings now were different. Their little group had fed hours ago on a bench beside a bus stop, and now, renewed hunger, and their aching feet in the new track shoes, were at the forefront of Andy's and Sheena's minds.

"Thank God we didna wear they boots Sandy brought," sighed Sheena.

"Ay, we'd have been murdered," said Andy. "I put them in the load. It was as well the lads came. We'd no have got far for a start, pushin' that lot. We'll be more used to it soon."

At last the grey and the brick and the concrete high-rise ebbed away, and in their place came the green and the yellow and the rust of the open countryside, made vivid in the last rays of sunlight. The children woke and whined, cold and estranged.

At a lay-by in the roadside, the Wolverines called a halt. "This'll dey," announced Big Mick. "There's wood an' water, an' a flat bit for the tent." It was the McBrides' first lesson in the great outdoors.

"Thanks a lot, lads," said Andy gratefully. "We'd never have got here without youse."

"Ach, wee'll no leave youse yet," said Mick. "We'd never make it back the night anyway. Wee'll make a bit of a fire to warm the kids, and get up the tent."

Sheena and Andy, aching in every limb, were only too pleased.

The Wolverines seemed to be enjoying themselves as they stormed the wood, vandalising the trees; whooping back with their looted branches; hacking at the logs with Sandy's axe; prancing and capering with liberated delight and boundless energy.

Even Helen and wee Jim caught their exuberant enthusiasm and, instructed by Noddy, began to gather dry twigs to start a blaze.

Andy got the tent off the cart and looked at it dubiously. He had had a practice at it, in Sandy's allotment, but it had seemed different now without the practical man at his elbow.

"Here, I'll give you a han' wi' that," said the solid, morose Jemmy. "See yon camp I wis at in the List D – me mate an me put up fuckin' twenty o' them. You hang on to them, an' reach them to me," and he handed Andy the bag of tent pegs.

Fergie was opening cans of beans.

"Away doon to the river and get water, Hen," he ordered, handing the kettle to Sheena. She hesitated, and then, with an apprehensive glance at the scars on his face and the knife in his belt, went, cautiously and clumsily feeling her way down the bank, shrieking as the pull of the water against the kettle took her by surprise. She brought the kettle back, and put it carefully on the fire beside the pot of beans.

An hour later, Andy sat over the great crackling fire, weighing it all up in a kind of wonder. It had really come off: they were on their way, they were out of the city, they were warm and fed, the kids were asleep. Sheena and the lads were singing and cracking jokes. The extent to which this state of affairs was due to Sandy's motivation and the Wolverines' help, he dimly acknowledged and accepted. Tomorrow he would be on his own, he thought drowsily. For now, his weary body cried out for sleep.

A hoarse shouting awoke the little encampment. It was Big Mick. "Jesus! Would you look who's here."

Andy heaved himself stiffly and heavily from the communal mattress to peer out of the tent. The Wolverines were awakening on the tarpaulin, beside the still-glowing embers of the fire. He looked, blinking in the clear morning light to where Mick was pointing. Across the road, under a tree, were two slight hunched-up figures, their faces glowing grotesquely pink in the morning sun, crouching together for warmth.

"God save us. Are they here? I'd forgotten them." He woke Sheena. "It's they Wierdies – the two that followed us yesterday. They're here."

"You're joking," said Sheena. "They're only bairns." She looked out. "If they've been there all night they'll be foundered. Hey… Youse," she beckoned, and the Wierdies shambled over, shivering, and pathetically edged to the fire.

Sheena scrambled out. "Poke it up a bit," she ordered the Wolverines, again sure of her ground and right to command.

"Gie them a cup of tea." She turned to the dejected pair. "What are youse doin' here?"

The Wierdies shuffled. "We couldn't get back when we followed youse, so we just came on," whined the taller of the two, inadequately.

"Well, these lads will take you back," stated Sheena firmly.

"Well, anyway, we don't want to go back," said the little one. "It's cold and there's nothing to eat. If we go to the north, we can catch fish and eat rabbits like he said you were going to dey." He looked appealingly at Andy.

"My god, that's all I need," said Sheena. "We canny feed you, that's for sure. We've only enough for a week or two ourselves, and we don't know what's after that."

Andy looked them over. He knew these two. They had run away from a children's home, where they had been dumped by social workers, and had not fitted in, even with the other Wierdies, who bullied them. They were the lowest in the pecking order.

Always soft, he said, "Maybe they could help to push the cart and gie a hand with the bairns."

The Wierdies nodded eagerly.

"Ye need yer heid examined," shouted Sheena angrily. "Push?! They're as thin as pencils anyway."

"Ach," said Andy, "you said yesel, they're only bairns."

Sheena was silent with indecision. "Weel, on your heid be it," she sniffed at last, huffily.

Big Mick was indignant too. "Youse are daft," he said, "but we're for away now."

The Wolverines had packed the tent, loaded the cart, and stamped out the fire. Their black leather jackets, and boots and chains and safety pins gleamed and glistened in the sun – commandoes in punk, ready for the fray.

"That was gallus," said Big Mick. "Maybe we'll come up again with our gear and see where you've got to and how youse is doing."

"Wee'll bake you a cake," laughed Sheena.

"Thanks again, lads," said Andy.

Sheena and Andy watched their rowdy departure until the lads disappeared over the horizon, still shouting insults and ribald remarks, but waving energetically every other minute until they were gone. For a time it seemed very quiet and lonely.

CHAPTER 4

Now, Andy pushed the cart, with Sheena helping as best she could, and the Wierdies and the children giggled and shoved and pushed each other as they skipped along the road, pulling at flowers and branches, and picking up pine cones till their pockets fairly burst with them.

The road narrowed and became rougher. It was hard going, but the sun was shining. They all had a go at pushing the cart up the little hills, and steadying it down the slopes. It was a grand new game. Then great tunnels of tall trees closed in on the road, their height and gloom making the children silent and wondering. Andy's and Sheena's feet, tender from yesterday's walk, began to feel on fire with pain. Their arms and shoulders ached as the push and pull of the cart went relentlessly on. The children whinged, "I want up... I want up... I want a ride." The bigger Wierdie gave him a pick-a-back, his thin body straining under the load.

Then a bend brought a break in the trees, and they were out of the shadows and into the warm sunshine. There was a dazzle of blue water, and a big, big mountain up behind – a postcard suddenly come to life.

The young ones ran forward eagerly. "There's boats; there's boats," shouted wee Jim.

"That'll be the Ben, and that's Loch Lomond," shouted Andy, made excited by the unexpectedness of the scene.

Uncomprehending of natural beauty, there was something which compelled them all to respond. "It's like a calendar, isn't it?" said Sheena.

She and Andy sat down in the sun on a mossy wall, content to rest.

"Yon's Loch Lomond," Andy said repeatedly to his unresponsive young, who were hurling stones at the moored boats.

"Dinnae do that!" said Sheena sharply, getting up. "We dinna want trouble. Wait. I'll show you how to skim them."

Remembering a childhood day at Millport, she picked up a flat stone and made it jump over the water, to the young ones' delight, and her own. Pleased, she came back to Andy, who was getting the primus ready for a cup of tea.

"I'm that stiff," said Andy.

"It's my feet's the worst," said Sheena. "Maybe I should put them in the water."

In no time they were all in the water, shrieking and splashing and clowning on the coarse gravelly sand, the cool clear water of the loch soothing and easing the hot swelling ache of their bruised feet. Helen and Jim were smiling and shouting, the tiredness of the walk forgotten, and the Wierdies seemed less like little old men, and more like normal children.

"Kettle's boiling," shouted Andy, and they all made a rush for the hot tea and the packet of chocolate biscuits which Sheena opened – a hoarded luxury she was glad, now, she had brought. Helen leaned against Andy contentedly, eyes shining, face coated in biscuit crumbs. "Isn't this great!" she sighed. Andy and Sheena smiled.

Andy looked at the Wierdies. The pink dye, without the daily injections, was beginning to fade. Pale faces with black circles round the eyes were emerging.

"Whit's your names?" he asked.

Before they could reply wee Jim spoke up. "That's Frankie, and that's Steve," he said, pointing. "They're my friends."

"No, they're mine," said Helen

"They're no," said Jim.

The Wierdies giggled.

"Well, whatever they are, they know hoo to eat," said Sheena, gathering up the remains of the biscuits. "We'd better get on a bit, if we're going, Andy."

As the afternoon wore on the sun disappeared, the blue loch became grey and ruffled as a little wind sprang up, and the Ben began to disappear behind the clouds. Then a thin, mean drizzle set in, dampening the spirits so raised by the lochside idyll of the morning.

The little party fell silent. They trailed on and on, each forward step an ordeal, as unaccustomed muscles screamed, and blisters rubbed against their shoes. The cart lurched through the potholes and the puddles.

Wee Jim, dragging behind with Steve, shouted. "My feet's wet. I want on the cart."

Sheena stopped. "Oh, Andy! I couldna push him too."

"Na," said Andy, "we'll have to stop the noo. We'll just walk on till we find a place."

They pushed on silently as the daylight ebbed and darkened. The rain was becoming heavy, and their clothes clung damply, though their bodies were still warm with the walking. The trees closed in again, giving dark dripping shelter. Frankie dived off the road to explore and returned.

"There's a wee space back in there," he ventured. "It would hold the tent and the cart."

Stumbling and slipping, they plunged into the wood, shoving and hauling the cart over the wet grass and the uneven ground. Fumbling at the ropes, they undid the tarpaulin and tumbled the tent onto the sodden ground.

"I want home," suddenly screamed wee Jim, in a hysteria of rage and misery.

"So do I," sobbed Helen. "I want pie and chips."

"Wheest, wheest," said Sheena, and she gave them the remains of the chocolate biscuits. Frankie and Steve looked on hungrily, but, for the moment, she had no pity for any but her own.

Andy flung the tent about, unconsciously compensating for his ineptitude by a frantic show of energy and noise.

"Hauld these," he yelled, hurling the pegs at Steve. "Help me put doon the tarpaulin first," he commanded Frankie.

After an eternity of hammering pegs and adjusting guys, the tent went up.

"Christ!" shrieked Sheena. "The door's opening into the bushes."

"It'll fuckin' have to do the noo," snarled Andy, beside himself with exhaustion and frustration.

Frankie seized the axe and hacked a rough way through for them, and they huddled together on the tarpaulin in the drooping tent – beginning to shiver as the cold and damp enveloped their exhausted bodies.

"Wee'll get out the primus and get a cup of tea," said Andy, forcibly calming himself. They set up the primus. He struck a match. It spluttered and went out, so did the next – and another, and another. All sodden in his pocket.

The children were sobbing hopelessly now, noses and eyes streaming, faces blotchy. Frank and Steve were visibly shaking, chilled to the bone in their flimsy, cut-out garments. There was a silence born of despair, then, "Andy, get oot the sleeping bags," said Sheena in a sharp voice, "and bring the old rug for they two."

Andy crept out into the dripping bushes and groped about, searching for the bags, thankfully dry, in one of Sandy's canvas sacks. The rain had slackened, but the wind was high and chill. They had pushed it too hard, he reflected. He had not left enough time to set up camp and get a fire going – but events had pushed them on. He peered around him in the dark, and then stared intently, becoming aware of a little glimmer of light further along the loch shore. He pushed through the bushes to look again, puzzled. It seemed to be nearly in the water – a boat perhaps, or another camper.

"Matches!" Maybe somebody there would give them some! He shoved the bags and rug into the tent, which still throbbed with sobs and snuffles and wee Jim's hysterical hiccups. Slipping and slithering over greasy rocks and tangled tree roots, he groped his way along the loch shore, towards the flickering light. As he drew nearer, he could see that it came from a fire, crackling cheerfully, and in its glow he took in what seemed to be an upturned van, and a long tunnel-like tent. Dark faces in the firelight. Tinkers, he realised suddenly.

He coughed nervously, to herald his approach, but realised they must have heard him a mile away. A man, two women and an indeterminable number of children were squatting on rubber tyres, round a great black pot, which hung from a bent hook on a tripod, almost obscuring the fire. It bubbled and hissed, and gave off steam, and a most mouthwatering, meaty smell.

"Hello. I came to see if you could let me have a couple of matches," said Andy, "tae light a primus. The wood is too wet up there for a fire. It's tae make the bairns a hot drink. We're camping," he added feebly.

"Bairns?" said the tinker, getting to his feet. "How many of you are there?"

Andy found himself blurting out his tale.

"Bring them down; bring them down," said the man urgently. "Sure there's plenty in the pot for all." His voice had the lilt and soft persuasion of Ireland. He reached into the tent, and lifted a hurricane lamp from a hook. "That'll see you back," he said.

"Well," said Sheena, when Andy told her of his excursion, "I never thought I'd see the day I'd be glad to sit down with the tinks, but I'd do anything for a warm-up."

Frankie and Steve were already out of the tent. Andy picked up the half-asleep Jim, and Helen hung onto Sheena.

The tinkers were ladling out great platefuls of stew when they reached the encampment. The woman handed it silently around. It tasted good. Andy was about to ask what it was, but changed his mind. It was maybe better not to know – might be hedgehog or something like that, and Helen and wee Jim would turn up their noses. They were all wolfing it down and the tinker woman looked pleased.

Andy turned to the man. "Are ye in scrap?" he inquired tentatively, nodding towards the old van and the tyres.

"Used to be," answered the tinker. "Stayed near the city in winter, and came here in the summer, but that's all over now.

No traffic on the roads, no need for scrap. We're back to the old ways." He nodded towards the perimeter of the fire and Andy, leaning forward, could discern a stack of half-finished baskets, a pile of besoms, and creepie stools.

"I'm going to do horn spoons when I get hold of a few antlers," he added. "I've got me faither's old moulds. We do a bit of sharpenen' too – round the farms. The childer make clothes-pegs."

Sheena was peering curiously into the long, tunnel tent, discovering that the framework was branches bent in a half loop, with a canvas cover slung across them. It looked neat and ordered; there were mattresses, and upended packing cases with pans and dishes and mugs stacked on them. At the back there was a little stove with a half-funnel going up through the roof.

"How many children have youse?" she asked the silent women, who had been regarding her closely. "Six," said one of the women. "Four mine, and two hers."

Sheena questioned no further. "These two are mine," she said putting an arm round the drowsy children. She told them about Frank and Steve, and their previous life in children's homes, and about how it had been in the city after the shutdown. The women, Mollie and Mary, talked of potato picking and the raspberry fields at Pitlochry. Mollie showed Sheena her tattooed arms with pride, and Sheena made Andy show them his. They all became friendly.

It was late, and the wind chill, when they rose to go.

"The lads can sleep here for the night. You'll not have much room for them up there, and they'll be warmer," said the man, whose name was Malachy.

In the morning the McBrides had the kettle on, and tea brewed, when Frankie and Steve appeared. "We've got ours," they said, "and these are for you – four fresh eggs. They've got hens over there in a wee pen."

"Hens," thought Andy. "We could keep hens when we get settled somewhere."

While they ate, he told them about the time he helped his granda with racing pigeons when he was a wee lad. He'd liked that. Ay, he could manage hens fine.

They were loading the cart, when Malachy pushed through the bushes, and addressed himself to Andy.

"I do be thinkin' now. The two big lads – my women said – they don't belong to you. I'll take them off your hands. Plenty they can do around here. I could be doing with more help. Mine are too young to do much yet."

Andy looked at Frank and Steve. They had drawn close together, and were looking at him with set, shut-in faces. Poor little buggers, he thought. Just handed about all their lives like bloody parcels. He looked at Sheena. Their food supply was going down fast – but her face gave no clue. He looked at the boys again and then said firmly, "Now, now, Malachy. It's OK. I'll just hing onto them. They're my responsibility noo."

He noticed that Sheena looked relieved, and the lads scampered off.

"Well now," said Malachy without further comment, looking at the cart. "Would you be interested in buying a lovely donkey?"

Andy gave a short laugh at the unexpected change of subject, and the ridiculous quality of the question. Then he remembered the burning feet and the strained muscles of yesterday.

"Are ye serious?" he enquired.

Wee Jim was jumping up and down chanting, "Buy a donkey, get a donkey, buy a donkey, daddy." The others started.

"Where is it, Malachy, and how much do ye want?" said Andy.

Malachy took him across the road and into a ramshackle shed. "She's a beautiful beast; gentle as a lamb and strong as a lion," he breathed. It was a travesty of an animal, even to Andy's inexperienced eye. Its legs were barely capable of holding its body up, never mind pulling a cart, but what did he have to lose? Money wasn't useful for much nowadays, and he'd saved a bit from the dole to bring with him.

He gave Malachy ten pounds and Malachy threw in an ancient harness made of bits of rope and old straps, with which he attached the beast to the cart. The children were ecstatic with delight, and the tinker family waved them off with warmth and good wishes.

"What an escapade," said Andy when they rounded the first bend. "Never did I think I'd be a horse owner."

"Well, there'll not be many rushing to put a bet on yon nag," said Sheena drily. "It's a right pied piper you're making o' yerself." She put a hand on his arm. "But ye did right to bring the lads wi' us. Yon tinks was kind enough, but it wouldn't have been right: ye need to be born to that way of going."

Andy nodded, pleased at her praise. There was a sense of shared satisfaction between them. The donkey, soon christened nothing more exotic than 'Neddy' by the children, pulled well despite his decrepit appearance, and Frank and Steve, appointing themselves as donkey boys, coaxed the younger ones to have rides on his back. Andy and Sheena, for the first time, were free to walk unencumbered.

CHAPTER 5

The day passed pleasantly enough, without a repeat of yesterday's rain. A couple of cyclists passed them with a word of greeting, bending low over their heavily loaded bikes. A turf cart passed going the other way, with its load of fuel for the hospitals.

About midday they reached an old inn by the roadside. Its door stood open. There were farm carts and bicycles outside and a noise of clattering crockery within. Most pubs, cafes and hotels in the city had shut down months ago – scarcity of food and no light or heat made service impossible – so Andy approached the door with hesitation. It was dark inside, though there were great log fires at each end of a big long room, blazing away in cavernous stone fireplaces. As his eyes became accustomed to the gloom he saw that he was in an old, old hostelry. The tables were beer kegs, and there was an iron candlestick on each one. There were muskets and targes and old brown, faded pictures on the walls. The old Scots songs were being churned out from a wind-up gramophone.

Andy approached a wee man in a kilt, with a kind face, who appeared to be the landlord.

"I've no food to spare," Andy was told, "but I can give you a big pot of tea."

"You've no a pint, I suppose?" said Andy, joking.

"Well," said the landlord, "I can let you have a glass of home-brew."

Andy grinned his surprise and delight and went out to usher in his waiting party, seating them on a bench at the fire. A row of hands were soon stretching out to the warm red glow, while a row of feet tapped in time to the music.

"Where have you come from?" said the wee man, coming round with the teapot. They told him.

"Ay, there was a lot came up when it first happened," he said. "It's thinned out a bit now, but I've a notion there'll be more before it's over. I don't see many coming back down, except the peat men, and the vegetable carts. They make big money in the city these days, though God knows, there's little to spend it on up here now. I'd rather have a sack of flour myself than the money. Our supply is very low. We'll have to see about grinding our own next year. Where are you heading for?"

"Fort William," said Andy, looking hard at him. This had been Sandy's idea – he had a notion it might be easier to find a place to settle when they got past there – and Andy was interested to see what the landlord thought.

"Ye've a bit to go yet, then," he said, "though it's a good time of year for travelling. There's some set out last autumn and got stuck on the moor in the snow. A couple died. But you'll need to go well past Fort William. They're having trouble feeding their own up there, you know, but you'll not be stuck for firewood.

Andy told him about the high-rise flats without light or heat or lifts.

"Then you've little to lose getting out of there," said the landlord. "Have you done much walking before?" Andy told him about Sandy and how the idea had germinated.

"Och," said the landlord, laughing, "I mind Sandy Wilson. A great fellow! He used to come in here many a time. Everybody on the road knew him: hikers, cyclists, tinkers. Many a crack I had with him."

Andy was pleased and intrigued to find, in this kindly man, a link with Sandy.

The landlord saw them to the door.

"Are your feet not sore in those soft shoes?" he queried, looking them over. Andy thought of the boots Sandy had provided for them, still in their cardboard box in the cart.

"We've boots in the load," he mumbled. "We'll have to get them out."

"Wear them a wee while every day, at first. You'll soon get the feel of them," advised the landlord.

The next time they stopped, Andy unwrapped the boots. Inside each was a pair of thick woollen socks. Sheena was dubious, and the children whined and girned, but he insisted that they try them. He put his feet in his own and then withdrew them, muttering. He groped in the toes and then laughed.

"Look. Look whit Sandy's put in the boots." Not paper, as he'd thought, but packets of seeds.

"Hooch," said Sheena, "does he think we're goin' to grow flowers?"

"No, no, it's vegetables, like he has in the allotment." Andy put them carefully back in the cardboard box.

"He was always deyin' things for 'ither folk," said Sheena.

"He was that," agreed Andy, thinking about Sandy as they trudged on, and he looked with concern and a new awareness at Frank and Steve in their worn-out garments and broken shoes. Sheena was coaxing Helen and Jim along in their new boots.

"Look. Clump, clump, clump. We're like Neddy now," she laughed.

She'd done well, he thought. She complained plenty, but she'd plenty of guts when her mind was made up. Even after last night's escapade, she'd never mentioned giving up. Fiercely protective as she was of Helen and Jim, he knew that much of her high spirits were for their benefit.

At the evening camp, again by the lochside, Andy unfolded the map for the first time. He lay flat on his stomach, and stared at the map, which he had spread out on the grass before him. He was bewildered. He had never owned an atlas. There had been some instruction at school, but he had never felt that map-reading had anything to offer him. Getting through school and out again with as little bother as possible had been his aim. Nothing he saw or did there seemed to relate to his way of life, except the woodworking class. He'd liked and understood that. He peered uncomprehendingly at the maze of lines, colours and names of places. Then, with a sense of achievement, he spotted GLASGOW. He put a pebble on this spot in case he would lose it, and perused further. Then he realised that the long, pale blue lung above it was LOCH LOMOND. Christ! Was that all the far they'd come? He looked about for Fort William. A long time it took, but he persisted. When he found it, he was horrified – away up there! Then, pleased with his prowess, he called Sheena and the young ones to look.

"See that blue bit?" he pointed, his great rough fingers scouring the map. "That's water. That's Loch Lomond, here, where we are the noo. See the stone? That's where Glasgow is." He did not dare show them Fort William yet. He refolded the map carefully and stowed it in his anorak pocket. He'd have another look tomorrow night, now that he'd got the hang of it.

CHAPTER 6

Every day, they learned something new, and were still to learn as the days passed. They knew how to choose a sheltered place to camp; how to keep wood and matches dry to start their fires; and how to cut heather for Frank and Steve, who now slept more comfortably under the tarpaulin in the angle of the upturned cart.

Every day their feet became tougher, their muscles harder, their stiffness in the morning less. Their faces were ruddy, beaten and burned by the wind and the sun. Their clothes smelled of wood smoke and they slept soundly at night. With the pure air and the exercise, their appetites became insatiable – a great source of worry to Andy and Sheena as they doled out their dwindling food supplies.

So far they had managed, eking out the beans and the corned beef with potatoes and eggs from the roadside farms and dwellings. But now they had come to the isolation of the open moor. They stared at great tracks of watery land stretching to the horizon, where they met wide expanses of open sky, unbroken by the outline of a house or bush.

The first day on the moor frightened and awed them with its bleak vastness, and left them prey to the wind. Great blasts caught them unawares, and buffeted and blew them around, like feathers.

Next day, the sun came out and all the patches of grey water reflected the sky, and became bright, shining blue. They made their camp early on a beach of coarse sand, and the children made castles and splashed in the water, while the adults unloaded the cart and sorted the stores.

"Andy," said Sheena, "did you know there's only four potatoes left?"

"Surely not!" said Andy in alarm. "What else have we?"

"Tea, and a wee tin of ham, and a turnip for Neddy." Andy's heart sank. They had not been prepared for the long trek through the barren, inhospitable moor, and there was no doubt that the appetites of the growing boys had severely strained their resources.

Sheena cooked the potatoes and sliced the meat thinly. She set the meagre offering on the plates, two without a potato. Frank and Steve reached forward eagerly with the others, and then realising, withdrew their hands. There was a pause, then Sheena said briskly, "Go on, lads, eat up. Andy and me isn't hungry the night." She did not look at him. Andy felt a great lump come into his throat.

He moved away from the little group, taking his map from his anorak and scanning it closely, until he was satisfied.

A bit further on, another little road led off this one, and a good bit down it, buildings were marked – maybe farms where he could buy potatoes and turnips to keep them going. It would be a detour on the journey, but worth it if they could obtain food. He'd get them up early in the morning, before they got too hungry, he thought.

Satisfied with his decision, he rejoined the others, and they lazed about their warm fire on the little lochan beach, sipping tea and watching the stars come out one by one in the evening sky.

"Twinkle, twinkle little star," droned wee Jim sleepily.

They all laughed.

"What's next?" said Sheena.

"I don't mind," said Jim. "I learnt it at school."

"He was only at school a week, Mammy," said Helen defensively.

"I know," said Sheena. "You say it then."

"I canna," muttered Helen.

"I can," said Steve. He chanted:

Twinkle, Twinkle, little star,
How I wonder what you are,
Up above the world so high,
Like a diamond in the sky.

"That's guid," said Sheena, and they all lay back in the heather and gazed up at the big, bright stars, set deep in the velvet sky.

By midday next day the little party dragged, tired, hungry, dispirited. They were coming to the fringes of the moor. Great black fearsome mountains loomed up, not solid and comfortable-looking like the Ben, which had dominated their days for so long, but threatening – black and jagged, hanging over them with menace.

The little road down the glen was narrow, winding and rough. It followed the course of a turbulent river, which exploded over great black boulders ironed smooth and shiny by its dash and vigour. It left in its wake peaty pools, topped with yellow froth, and linked by noisy waterfalls.

The mountains packed in closely, overwhelming the little party. The dragging trailing noise of their boots on the road, and the silence, indicated their weariness.

They plodded on until wee Jim sat down suddenly. "I'm too tired," he said woefully.

Frank and Steve rushed to pick him up. "Put him on the cart," said Andy. He had been anxious not to overtax the half-starved Neddy but the road was going downhill all the way. "We should be at the house in no time." He felt a little clutch of fear as he spoke, for he knew from the map that the road led nowhere. What if the houses were empty? So far, there was no sign of cultivation. All was barren deer forest, apart from the dense little clumps of forestry pine which fringed the road. "This is Scotland, no Ethiopia," he thought grimly. "We canna starve."

They struggled on, increasingly weak and dejected until the wild mountain country began to show signs of man's presence and attempts at taming it: first a wooden bridge, then a high deer fence, then signs which read: PRIVATE FISHING. Then, as they rounded a bend, they could see below them a great grey ugly house with tall chimneys, sprawled out across the valley floor. It was almost cut off by the ox-bow of the river, and approached from the road by a bridge. Smoke was coming from the chimney, and gradually the noise of human presence reached them. Wood was being sawed, dogs barked, and there were far-off voices. In their enthusiasm and relief the little party almost ran the last half-mile – Neddy's hooves and the boots clattering, and the wheels of the cart bumping on the rough surface – until they pulled up short before two high corrugated-iron gates, surmounted by a frieze of barbed wire.

Andy knocked loudly with his stick.

"Hi!" he shouted. "Anybody there?"

There was a silence. All activity on the other side ceased. After a minute the gates were forced open a crack, and a bearded face topped by a deerstalker hat surveyed them. "What is it?" was the greeting.

Andy told him what it was, and the face withdrew. Andy grimaced his satisfaction to the others, and they waited, expectantly. The gate did not reopen but there was a sound of firm, approaching footsteps. Then a loud voice, rich and fruity as a bag of plums, arose above the corrugated iron and the barbed wire and assailed them. "We have nothing here for anyone. Sorry, sorry. Afraid you must move on. Best to go back to the main road, my man."

"There's six of us," shouted Andy, in great alarm. "Four children. They haven' eaten a bite today."

"Sorry, sorry," said the voice. "Can't make exceptions. Must conserve our resources. Mouths to feed here, you know." The feet walked away on the other side.

Maybe they have nothing, thought Andy bitterly, but they could have opened the gate to say it. They walked numbly on down the hill, simply because they did not know what else to do. At the foot they stopped.

"We'll make a wee fire and get a cup of tea," said Sheena bravely.

While she prepared it, Andy wandered up a little rise, and looked back at the great house. From here he could see the doors and windows of the back premises. There was a kitchen garden with a wall around it – full of vegetables. He could see hens. A bitter, burning anger consumed him. He thought of the tinker sharing his pot, of Sheena giving her potato to the lads, and this lot with their 'private fishing', and their corrugated door 'conserving their resources'.

He went back to his listless, exhausted family and the little group dozed fitfully around the fire. They were awakened by the sound of barking dogs, and Andy went again up the little hill to look out.

The deerstalker hat had come out of the back door, and the dogs rushed, barking, around him. He went down the garden into a little hut with a tall roof. He came back out with something large in his hands and, using a knife, cut chunks off and threw it to the dogs. Andy was angry as he had never been angry before – murderously angry. Food for dogs, and none for starving children.

Then he calmed. He looked intently and carefully at the scene – at the river, the garden, the wall, the back door of the house – and he made his plans. He said nothing of them to the little company around the fire.

"We'll move further down the glen, and find a more sheltered spot to camp," he said quietly. "Maybe we can do a spot of fishing."

Wee Jim was whimpering and moaning with hunger, two big tears were stealing silently down Helen's cheeks, and Frank and Steve looked tired and drawn. He expected, at any minute, Sheena to accuse him of getting them all into this, but she did not.

He found a spot well away from the road, behind a thicket of trees, and drew Frank, the older of the two lads, aside. "When the others are sleeping, come with me."

Later, he shook him awake, and on the way up the road, he outlined his plan. A quarter of a mile below the great house they stepped into the icy, turbulent river; not deep, but strong and powerful, dragging their feet from under them as they jumped and slipped and grabbed their way over the smooth rocks, scrambling up the slippery grass bank of the other side. They followed the river up, until they came to the walled garden. Andy whispered his instructions to Frank, who silently disappeared into the darkness. His life with the Wierdies had accustomed him to this sort of undertaking – in a different setting.

Andy scaled the wall, and dropped down among the vegetables. Groping in the dark, he half filled his rucksack, pausing now and then to listen intently. Then he made for the wooden hut. He tried the door cautiously. It was open, but it dragged on its hinges, grinding and creaking. He shoved it half open, and edged inside. Something bumped against him, moist and smelly, and he exclaimed involuntarily. He struck a match, and then smiled grimly, as he surveyed the carcasses swinging from the roof on great hooks.

Our own resources, the miserable old beggar, he thought, slashing away with his knife to dislodge a great hunk of venison. Then – what he had feared. A sudden, sharp dog yelp, and then a whole chorus of barking. They must have heard the door shoved open, and sensed a stranger. A window opened, and then the back door. Feet on the gravel, coming close. Andy stepped outside, and waited, flattening himself against the hut. Then, in the distance – a great sound of breaking glass soon followed by a commotion of barking dogs, running feet and hoarse shouts, all diminishing as the noise of the glass drew them off towards the front of the house.

"Good lad, Frankie," Andy grinned, as he flung himself over the wall, grateful for his old army training and exhilarated with the success of his enterprise. Andy had never stolen before, but he felt no guilt whatsoever – only the primitive instincts of a hunter providing for his tribe. It seemed as fair a game as the deer hunting of the big house.

He met Frankie back on the road, and they inspected the spoils with satisfaction. On the way back to the camp, their exuberance became tinged with unease as they realised they were cut off at the head of the glen, and that to get back to the main road they would have to re-pass the big house. They could climb above it at night, but what about the cart, so vital to their expedition?

"We'll have to move further on and away from the house," said Andy. "They'll be after us at first light."

He roused the sleepers with promise of the food to come, threw a turnip to Neddy, and led them, grumbling and half conscious, on into the night.

The first rays of morning light were putting long fingers into the grey as they neared the end of the glen. The air smelled and tasted different, for here, where the peaty river met the long fiord-like loch, the salt water mingled with the fresh and brought the smell of the sea far up into the hills.

Up above the road, on a flat area, Andy saw the other building he had looked at on the map – a little house. It might be empty, he speculated, considering the tangle of derelict buildings on the shore: an old boathouse, a roofless bothy, an outhouse – relicts of a former community. If it was empty, they could shelter and sleep. He went up the path and peered in the window. No such luck – a red glow came from a big Aga cooker. Before it sat a row of sleek, well-fed cats.

Then a dog barked. Andy felt more than sick of antagonistic dogs. A woman's voice shouted "Who's that?" then "Be off with you; we want no strangers here." The curtains were pulled in his face. Aye, a kick for the stranger at your gates, and food for your cats and dogs, thought Andy as he stumbled down the path. In desperation, he pushed his way into the outhouse on the roadside

– an old stable, it appeared, but there was fresh straw on the floor. A couple of hens scattered out, flapping and croaking wildly in their disturbance.

Andy pulled his family inside, shut the door, wrapped them in the rugs and bags, and they all slept, motionless with exhaustion.

Sheena was awakened first by a small noise and, struggling to sit up, saw a young lad surveying them from the partially opened door. Alarmed by her awakening, he fled. She heard the gate bang, then the house door. She lay down again, too weak and despondent to care.

Probably come and throw us out soon, she thought wearily.

She felt ill with hunger. They would need time to cook the venison, and potatoes and carrots Andy had brought. She had been momentarily horrified at the account of the expedition to the big house, then past caring what happened as long as they could all eat again.

In the house up above, the door banged again, then the opening in the stable door darkened, and a woman stood there.

"I didna know there was bairns," she said abruptly, and set a large steaming platter on the floor – hot food, whatever it was! She beckoned the lad behind her – the lad whom Sheena had seen earlier – and he set down a can of milk. Both departed as quickly as they had come.

The others, awakening, stared incredulously at the salmon, potatoes and hard-boiled eggs which filled the dish to overflowing. Then mouths and their stomachs filled before they spoke.

"Some breakfast," laughed Andy, almost delirious with surprise and relief.

Soon Andy went up to the house to thank the woman. He recounted the events of the previous day, leading up to his encounter at the gates of the big house.

"Oh," she said slowly. "It doesn't surprise me any. They came up from London – the 'chappies', we call them – when the shutdown was threatened, and while there was still petrol to be had. Brought a lot of their friends with them. I work for them; it keeps a roof over our heads in this glen. I don't miss any washing machines or electric light for I never had any, but the chappies and their wives can't manage without service. I light the fires, do the lamps, cook and clean for them. They never did anything to earn that place; it was bought in Queen Victoria's time, and handed on to them. They were only here a couple of months in the year until the shutdown happened, and they employed very few folk. It's always been 'private', 'keep off', 'keep out', where they're concerned. But now they've got venison, sheep on the mountain, and fish in the river, when other folk are suffering."

Andy heard her out, and then told her the rest of last night's story, including the stone through the window.

"Oh," she cried uneasily. "You'd best be off then. They have bicycles. The keeper can be down here in no time."

Then a thought struck her, and she called agitatedly to the young lad. "Roddie! The boat. You could take these folks down the loch, and put them off where they could take the forestry track back to the road. That way," – she turned to Andy – "you'll not have to pass the house—"

"But we have the cart," Sheena interrupted.

"Oh, we can upend that and get it in the boat," the lady said firmly, "and the donkey can swim behind, if he's tied on." She was speaking abruptly again, and Andy had the idea she could not wait to get them off the premises. It would probably be as much as her job was worth, if she was caught harbouring them. Natural hospitality had to toe the line when it came to harsh economic realities. The woman took Neddy's head, and led the little procession to the tumbledown pier.

"Where is it you're heading for, anyway?" she queried. A look of astonishment came over her face when Andy said they didn't know.

"Well, it will not be hereabouts, while that lot up there are in charge." She nodded in the direction of the big house. She was silent for a moment, thinking, before saying, "My father was a shepherd, and we moved about all over the place. I mind a village out on the coast where there were good, stout houses. I've heard they're all empty now. They'd be no landowners to bother you there. There's good fishing, and a bit of grazing land; and the folk, if there are any left, would be friendly, unless they're overrun with bodies like you. You can mention my name if you get there." She added, "It's Morag McKay."

Andy pulled out the map and, with Morag's help, traced the way to the village, away to the west of Fort William. It was wild, rough, lonely country, Morag said.

Roddie packed the boat with their meagre possessions, helped by the children, who had forgotten the misery and hunger of yesterday, and were laughing and chatting in the warm sunshine.

As they took their leave, Morag pressed a bundle she had brought, into Frankie's hands. "A couple of old jerseys to keep out the cold," she said. They waved to her from the boat, but she was already on her way back to the croft.

CHAPTER 7

The journey down the loch was full of wonder and astonishment. The children hung over the side of the boat, exclaiming about the depth of the clear water and the white sand glimmering below. They splashed poor Neddy, who swam gamely behind. Andy and Sheena gazed at the little secret bays of the loch shore, and the haze of the bluebells and the dazzling yellow gorse; and the rhododendrons half swallowing up the mountainside in wave after wave of bright purple. Roddie pointed out the stags watching them motionless from the old woods. A few miles down the loch, he pulled the boat into a little bay, and they stepped out into a larch wood carpeted with primroses. They all unloaded the boat, and waved Roddie off.

"Some day," called Sheena, "we'll come back and see you, and bring you the biggest bag of sweeties you ever saw."

The shy Roddie grinned and nodded.

That night they cooked the venison over their open fire, and boiled the vegetables in the big pot. They slept among the primroses and soft ferns, and listened to the gentle lapping of the water. Frank and Steve were warm, for once, in their thick, hand-knitted sweaters.

Next day, they took the forest track to the main road, and headed north again.

Spring was merging into summer when they reached Fort William. The roads were dusty and hot, but the fields blazed with dandelions and buttercups, and they cooled their feet in the long grasses.

On the edge of the town, Andy made enquiries about what could be obtained in the way of food supplies, and was directed to the police station for emergency ration cards.

Food was getting very tight, the friendly policeman told him. Tinned stuff was disappearing altogether, and sugar supplies were on the wane. But up here, everyone was growing what they could, and keeping goats and chickens and grinding flour; so it was people on the move from the cities, like himself, who were suffering most. He'd heard it was very bad now in Glasgow, with the looting, and the old and the very young were dying like flies over the winter.

Andy remembered his own desperation at the big house in the glen.

He stocked up as best he could with the motley selection of food available, then took Frank and Steve to a camping store to enquire about boots to replace their tattered, flapping track shoes.

"It's as well it's the smaller sizes you want," said the young chap at the counter. "It's been like the gold rush here the past months. We've hardly anything left. I'll have to have a go at the boot-making myself – and why not?" He laughed. "It'll pass the winter."

A week or so later, they reached the road end that Morag McKay had indicated on the map – a long twisting road, it appeared – opening into a wide valley as it neared the sea. It was in this valley that the deserted village was marked, a good ten miles off the main road.

"We'll go doon a bit and find a sheltered place for the night," said Andy.

Some miles further, they reached the brow of the hill and stood, gazing anxiously down, in the waning evening light.

Far off they could see the sea, and the dim, soft shapes of islands. The bottom of the valley seemed greener than the barren deer forest where they stood. Frank pointed out what seemed to be a house – a gleam of white in a cluster of trees. Tomorrow they would know if this was to be the end of their wanderings.

Andy and Sheena slept fitfully, with little whispered conversations throughout the night.

"What if it's nae guid?" asked Sheena.

"Well, we'll just go on again," said Andy. "We've done it before."

"Och, I'd like to get dug in somewhere before winter," said Sheena anxiously. "We'd need to get a house fixed up, and food gathered in. I know fine it'll be a tough time for us; in summer it's easier to manage."

Next morning, as they neared the end of the valley, evidence of an earlier settlement was everywhere: in the tumbled stone walls, almost hidden by the tangle of brambles and honeysuckle and wild roses which ran riot over them; in the humpy outlines of old rigs; and a spout projecting where a gush of water cascaded from the hillside. There were rowan trees, and young birch and larch.

The grassy lane, which the twisting road had now become, forked steeply up to the right. This must be the way up to the house they had glimpsed last night, but the deserted village would be to the left, on the way down to the sea.

"Come on, folks," urged Andy. "Keep going. You can have a play on the sand in a wee while." He did not want to raise their expectations beyond that.

Another turn in the lane, and they were confronted by a sturdy little grey stone house which, from its very sharp-pointed gable, asphalt playground, and grey stone wall around it, they knew to be the old schoolhouse. From its chimney a long thin streak of smoke issued straight up into the bright air.

Andy and Sheena were instantly alarmed. This place was inhabited. People were here before them. "We'd best see what the score is before we go any further," said Andy heavily.

He and Sheena approached the open door with apprehension. A smell of baking bread came from within. They knocked tentatively and timidly. "Hullo?" called a surprised voice. A chair scraped on a stone floor; footsteps, and a young woman appeared on the threshold.

Andy and Sheena stared, both struck by the beauty that confronted them – long, thick, corn-coloured plaits of hair, great blue eyes, white teeth and a wide, sweet smile. In her blue dress she looked like a child's doll in a toyshop.

Andy stammered, "We came down here… We were given the name of this place. We're looking for somewhere to stay. We've walked from Glasgow."

Sheena took over. "A woman called Morag McKay sent us here. Do you know her?"

"No," said the young woman. "We have not been here very long, but old Kezia up on the hill may know. She and Angus, her husband, are the only ones left here." She spoke slowly and clearly, with a slight foreign accent.

"Are there other new people?" asked Andy.

"No. Only my friend Peter and myself. He is collecting wood down on the beach. There are many empty houses down there." She looked at them carefully, and then smiled again. "I am glad people with children have come. My name is Gudrun. You must be tired; it is a long way down from the main road. Come in and have something to eat and drink."

She drew them into a large room, where a peat fire burned brightly, its smell mingling with the perfume from the great pots of honeysuckle and wild roses on the window sills.

Andy went over to unharness Neddy, and Sheena and the children looked curiously around the room, which was sparsely furnished with old dark wooden school furniture, but bright and cheerful. A blue checked cloth was on the table, there were plates and mugs on the dresser, and there were shelves full of books.

"It's nice in here, Mammy," whispered Helen. "She's like a fairy princess, isn't she?"

Gudrun brought them scones fresh from the girdle over the fire, and a pot of gooseberry jelly. She filled their mugs from a big brown teapot.

"I'm still practising with those," she laughed, nodding at the scones. "Kezia showed me how to use the girdle."

"I mind my gran used one of those," said Sheena.

Tongues loosened, and they told her the story of their travels.

"And how long have you been here?" quizzed Sheena.

"I camped here with Peter about two years ago," said Gudrun. "We became friendly with Kezia and Angus, so when things began to get difficult after the shutdown, we took the train from London to Fort William – one of the last trains, I think it was – and then we walked here. Kezia and Angus were glad to have company in the glen. They are old. Angus had a stroke and cannot work about the croft any more. They had two sons, but one was killed in the war, and the other drowned when his fishing boat went down. They teach us about the land, and the animals and the fishing, and the old ways of doing things." She stood up suddenly. "Look. There's Peter."

A bearded young man was coming quickly up the path, looking curiously at Neddy and the children, who had drifted outside to play. After Gudrun's quick explanation, he greeted them warmly. "There are houses still in fair condition down on the shore," he told them. "Nicer view than this, too. We fancied them ourselves, but this one had the best roof, and the old folk like to see our lamp in the window at night."

CHAPTER 8

Andy and Sheena felt a great sense of relief. Everything suddenly seemed right and possible. At last they could stop and make a home and think about the future. Now their minds and energies must turn in another direction.

They had liked instantly the gentle, smiling Gudrun, Peter seemed all right, and they liked the sound of the old folks up above. They smiled and chatted, enjoying the simple pleasure of sitting on chairs at a table again.

"Right, Andy," said Peter at last. "Maybe we should go to the shore and look at the houses."

They all went down the little loaning behind the schoolhouse. It wound through a hazel wood, and onto what Gudrun and Peter called the machair – a sandy meadow behind the beach, its short green grass almost hidden in the bright profusion of wild flowers. The machair fringed a deep bay with a white sandy beach, and on the far side they could see a little street of grey, stone houses – five or six in all – almost roofless. The children were already half way across the bay, shouting and whooping, to choose their home. Andy and Sheena became excited too, as laughing, out of breath, they followed the children's headlong flight across the sands.

"We never thought we'd get to choose our own house," Andy joked.

Peter pointed out to one with a rudimentary roof. "Gudrun and I had our eye on that," he said.

Sheena became immediately practical.

"Well – it'll take a while to get that place sorted," she pronounced, looking askance at the broken floorboards, and animal droppings, and the age-old cobwebs which festooned the ancient window frames and hung from the rafters. A great black pot hung from the swey in the sooty fireplace. Peering up, they could see the little white fleecy clouds through the broken beams.

"We will all help," said Gudrun. "It will be fun if we do it together. The little ones can sleep in our house in the meantime."

"Frank and Steve can have our tent," added Peter.

Andy tramped about outside, hands in pockets – looking. There was plenty of wood: great spars washed up on the beach, fish boxes and planks too, and more caught up on the jagged rocks beyond. There were reasonable slates lying about in some of the other houses – a job for Frank and Steve to find the best ones, he decided.

He felt confident and eager to start, but today was a holiday. They had arrived at their new home!

"We will have to take you up to Kezia and Angus," said Peter. "They will know strangers have arrived, and they will be anxious. We were often afraid of people coming who might take advantage. I'll go ahead and tell them about you."

Kezia was waiting at the door for them as they struggled up the steep slope. She was a tall, straight, strong-looking woman, her white hair framing a weather-beaten face. Her black dress and black boots were relieved by a long white apron. Her eyes were bright and searching and she looked fierce, but spoke gently.

"Come away in," she urged, shaking hands with each in turn as they crossed the threshold.

A little, wizened old man, propped up by pillows, greeted them cheerily from a box-bed, which ran along the back wall of the warm kitchen.

"My, my," he joked. "A real Sunday excursion, this! We haven't seen so many folk for years and years."

The children giggled.

Sheena and Andy sat on the hard, wooden, kitchen chairs, and again retold their story. Kezia's bright eyes looked intently at them, and old Angus nodded occasionally as the tale unfolded.

"And we'd like to set up here, if you'll all have us," finished Andy, with an encompassing glance at Gudrun and Peter.

There was only a short wait, while Kezia and Angus stared first at the floor, then at each other in unspoken understanding.

"Let Frank and Steve stay here," said Kezia firmly. "There's bedrooms in the loft that haven't been used for quite a long time. It will be good to have young folk about the place again. We applied to the welfare to foster some a few years back, but we didnae get any." She gave a bitter laugh. "They thought we would exploit them, use them as farm servants; and so we would have worked them hard, but they'd have had a good clean home, good food and kindly treatment. Might have been better than what these laddies put up with. Anyway, we'd like them to bide here for a bit. They can help you to fix up your house, and maybe give Angus and me a hand about the place. We'll teach them as we go, and maybe have a bit of fun in the doing too. We lost our own laddies, you see." She winked at Frank and Steve, who were looking apprehensive at the new development, but this time Andy and Sheena had no qualms about handing them over.

CHAPTER 9

S o, a new order of living and working began for the little community – those already established, and the newcomers to the glen.

The long summer days never seemed long enough for the tasks to be carried out in them. The little glen rang with the sounds of hammering and sawing, intermingled with the noise of children's games and shouts and laughter.

The gleam of Kezia's white apron was often to be seen as she stood at her door, listening and savouring the new life and activity around her. One morning a chair was placed at the door, and Frank and Steve appeared, supporting Angus between them. From then on, on sunny mornings, the chair went further and further, Angus dictating its movements, until at last he was there in the midst of them all, instructing, showing, ordering, planning for the winter ahead.

Some mornings they went higher up, onto the moor among the little black pools and the white bog cotton, and they cut and turned and stacked the peats – for the winter fires. In the afternoons the men and boys worked on the house. The women cooked, baked, washed and made jam together, Kezia initiating them into the mysteries of cooking on the swey, with the girdle and the great black pots. Gudrun, who liked working with wood, would sometimes lose patience with housework, and be off to help Andy with his new fireplace and window frames, but Sheena was well content with Kezia's company, and they took care of the hens and the vegetable garden together.

Andy and Peter were less compatible, Peter's philosophical arguments being for the most part lost on Andy, and the latter's Glasgow patter irritating Peter at times, but both worked hard to bring the peat down, and Andy was grateful for the hours Peter put in on the house.

Some days Gudrun would come out laden with easel, paints and picnic basket, and disappear for the day, followed closely by Helen, who would come home proudly displaying her little paintings of flowers and boats, and seals lying up on rocks.

"Them's bonnie flowers," said Sheena, looking through them.

"That's foxgloves and dog roses," said Helen, "and that's the flowers on the machair, and, see, I've put our new house on this one."

Every night Frank and Steve took wee Jim down to the rock pools, and he would stagger home laden with bucketfuls of little green crabs and shrimps, and a very occasional fish.

So the days passed – busy, some exhausting, but never boring as they cut, dug, sawed and sowed their way towards the winter months. The little house became wind- and rainproof as the men clambered over the roof, hoisting the newly sawn beams into place, and nailing and hammering in the slates. The inside became increasingly brighter as Sheena and Gudrun scrubbed and scraped and scoured. The grimy windowpanes became clear and glistening, letting the sunshine flood into the little rooms.

One memorable day, Sheena put up her carefully ironed curtains and they lit a fire in the hearth. They brought a spare table from the schoolhouse. Kezia had produced a bed spring from an outhouse; and fish boxes from the beach would serve as furniture in the meantime. Andy planned to spend part of the winter making what was necessary, and he looked forward to it.

The golden days of summer shortened, and they began to gather around the hearth fires in the evenings – sometimes up the hill with Kezia and Angus, sometimes at the schoolhouse, and sometimes at Andy and Sheena's little home.

Andy was carried away with his woodworkings, designing furniture for his own and the other houses, and talking excitedly about making a boat to replace Angus's old one down on the beach. The old man was immediately interested, and both had long intense conversations about ways and means, while the women knitted and Peter read to the children.

One afternoon in early autumn, Andy and Peter went off to the shore to bring back spars jammed in the outer rocks. Gudrun, with Helen, as usual, at her heels, set off to paint, while Sheena took wee Jim up to Kezia's for a knitting session. Between them they meant to see to it that all the little clan had warm jerseys, caps, gloves and socks for the coming winter.

The glen was quiet, peaceful, beautiful in the mellow autumn sunlight. The men finished their work on the shore, and sat chatting quietly on the rocks as the sun lowered itself slowly into the sea, flecking the surface with silver and pink and gold.

Suddenly, into the stillness came a high-pitched scream, with another and another. "Something's wrong," shouted Peter as they leapt up. "That's not the children."

Andy was already running. As they crossed the bay, a shot rang out.

"Oh, God!" cried Andy, "Whit's that?" His heart was pounding.

"Look," panted Peter, as they crashed round the bend towards the little schoolhouse. He pointed up to where old Kezia was standing, a smoking rifle in her hands. She was shouting something and Steve was beside her, shouting too, and pointing towards the woods at the bottom of the lane. They ran as directed – not knowing what for. Andy stumbled first over Gudrun's easel, then saw Helen's little pictures scattered across the path. Now he could hear Helen's sobs. They rushed into the trees.

In a clearing Gudrun stood, back to a tree, a branch in her hand, her dress torn, her hair dishevelled, her face bleeding, desperately lashing out at two dark, sturdy, attacking figures. Helen cowered on the ground, hands over her head, moaning and sobbing.

Andy and Peter were on the attackers in an instant, tearing them back, thumping, hammering, throwing them to the ground. The wood resounded with cracking branches, muffled shouts, and cries of rage and pain. Frank and Steve had dashed to help too, and between them all they flattened the assailants on the ground, faces down and thrashing wildly.

Andy ran to the shaking Helen and held her close. "We were painting in the meadow," she sobbed, "and they jumped at us. They knocked Gudrun down and kissed her, and pulled at her dress." Her voice rose to a shriek. "Gudrun screamed and screamed, and then Kezia fired her gun, and we got away into the wood, and then they came after us again." She was trembling all over with shock and fright. Gudrun was deathly pale but calm as Sheena led her away from the scene.

An inarticulate sound from Steve and an urgent "Andy, look!" from Frank drew his attention from Helen, and he stared in disbelief as the defeated attackers began to struggle to their feet. It was Big Mick and Jemmy!

Andy was speechless, as rage, disgust, astonishment and uncertainty in turn took possession of his feelings.

"We didn't mean any harm," muttered Big Mick, eyeing them uncertainly.

"Not likely," snarled Peter, ready to throttle him with his bare hands.

Andy was confused. He needed time to think. He felt an obligation to Mick and Jemmy, who had launched them on the enterprise which led them to this glen. He knew their background, and could understand their behaviour. Girls were fair game to them, and most could give as good as they got, but wee Helen and Gudrun – they could not handle this.

He looked at the tight-lipped Peter.

"I'll need to talk to you," he said. "We'll put these two in the old stable, and lock the door on them, for now."

"Don't know whit all the fuss is about," snarled Jemmy as they were hauled away.

Andy and Peter went to Kezia and Angus's house, where Gudrun's face was being bathed, and Kezia was comforting them all with pots of tea.

They began to recover, and discuss what had happened.

Andy told them about the Wolverines, and the kind of life they had led, and their unexpected assistance to his family. There was a silence. Gudrun was the first to speak.

"We must give them a chance," she said gently. "You must not worry; I am not upset any more, nor, indeed, afraid of them. It was all so unexpected: nothing has bothered us here before." They all stared at her, astonished.

"They'd best bide here – that's if they've a mind to bide at all," said Angus. "They can go up the stair with the lads. That way I can watch what they're up to, night and day, till we see how they shape."

So it was agreed, but a new element had come into the little community, and an awareness of violence and evil, apprehension, a need to distrust and be watchful.

The subdued Mick and Jemmy told Andy they had decided to take to the road when the going became too hard in the city and, anyway, they fancied the adventure after their preliminary excursion with Andy and Sheena. The turf men had told them where the McBrides had settled. They had come down the glen and found Gudrun and – as Andy recognised – a pretty girl was fair game in their society.

Peter, Angus and Andy put the terms to them: if they behaved and fitted in and worked well with the rest they could stay on a trial run. "Step out of line," said Peter firmly, "and you're on your way."

"Don't know if we want to stay anyway," grumped Jemmy. But they did.

CHAPTER 10

By the end of the autumn, neat stacks of turf and piles of chopped wood were to be seen around the inhabited houses. The little vegetable gardens were flourishing, the hens were laying well and the children were thriving. Andy's slack belly had long since disappeared, and he looked strong and tanned. Scrawny little Sheena, on the other hand, had filled out and looked almost pretty.

On a golden afternoon Gudrun and Sheena sat in the heather, knitting, taking advantage of the warm sunshine, for the mornings and evenings had become sharp and frosty, heralding the onset of winter.

The menfolk were making the most of it too, all down on the shore, banging away at the new boat, with old Angus in his chair to supervise operations. Helen, with wee Jim in tow to hold the can, had gone to pick blackberries for Kezia somewhere along the burn.

The young women talked idly at intervals, enjoying the sun and unexpected hours of peace and quiet.

"The days are fair drawing in," said Sheena. "What do you think it will be like here in winter, Gudrun?"

"Oh, not too bad," was the reply. "We have plenty of fuel, and the houses are sound now. We won't have as much food as in summer, but we've the goat's milk, and the hens, and potatoes… We can manage till the spring and then plant more for next year. People managed like this in the old days, you know. We just have to go back a bit."

Sheena turned this over. It had never occurred to her to think about a time when people knew no other way of life but this. To her, they were making the best of the situation, and she had not visualised a previous way of life – or indeed looked much into the future.

"In some ways," said Gudrun, half to herself, "I'm not sorry the shutdown happened. I know time cannot stand still, and we must make changes, and try out new inventions. So much of what has been done is good, but somehow ordinary people got left out. Man was alienated by the machine takeover, becoming almost a machine himself. People were too dependent on mechanical things, and when it all packed up, left helpless, all the old skills almost lost." She turned to the bewildered Sheena. "I know we must make progress, but this crisis has given people time to think about it all – perhaps to discard what was bad, like too many people living in too many cities – and relearn some of the good things that were lost. We are lucky to be in this place, and to have Kezia and Angus to teach us."

Sheena struggled to understand what she called Gudrun's 'notions'. "Well," she said, "I'm never fed up or lonely here, that's for sure. We have a hoose of our own, and I never thought we'd have that, and," she summed up with sudden realisation, "I'd rather sit here in the sun crackin' to you, than be trailing around the supermarket or sittin' in the flat."

Both fell silent, preoccupied with their thoughts. Their peace was broken by the appearance of a frantic little figure on the horizon, running, waving his arms wildly. As he drew nearer, the knitters could hear his anguished howls. What a wee hysteric that one is! Sheena thought with amusement, as she viewed Jim's red, contorted little face approaching. His voice reached them. "Mammy! Mammy! Gudrun! Helen's fallen down the waterfall. She's drowning."

Gudrun was up in a flash of gold hair and blue dress, racing across the meadow. Sheena followed, less fleetly, heart thumping and legs weak.

The fall poured over a jumble of grey rocks, into a deep, frothy pool. Sheena and Gudrun clawed through the tangle of bramble bushes which had attracted the children to this forbidden, gloomy spot. Their eyes raked the peaty water.

"There!" shouted Sheena, as a little white face and wet plastered hair swirled into view, and vanished again.

Gudrun dived, searched, and at last surfaced, clutching Helen.

"Get out onto that rock, Sheena," Gudrun shrieked above the noise of the fall. "I'll push her to you."

Sheena didn't hesitate, jumping, clutching, grabbing her way over the slithery rocks, hauling, pulling the heavy, sodden little body, as Gudrun pushed it from the water.

"Jim, run for Kezia," she screamed at the frightened little face above her. The crouching child turned, and scrambled up the bank, dislodging a large stone on the edge in his terrified progress. The stone rattled down the rocks, bounced off a large boulder, and fell with force into the pool, striking Gudrun on the side of the head.

Her grip on Helen loosened and she sank backwards into the pool.

"Oh, Gudrun, Gudrun! Oh, God, Oh, God!" Sheena sobbed hysterically, as, arm and shoulder muscles straining in agony, she struggled to keep Helen's shoulders above water. Powerless, she watched as Gudrun was drawn under the fall, tossed out again, and again, the gold hair streaming out behind her, then coiling about her throat. Sheena closed her eyes and held on numbly and dumbly, agony of mind and body making her almost beyond feeling.

At last there was a shout on the bank, and dimly she saw a flash of white apron. She could just hear Kezia's voice. "Hing on, Lassie, hing on a wee." She was aware of Gudrun being pulled from the water, then Helen being taken from her, and Kezia stooped, working over them. She struggled to them. "Take over Helen," said Kezia. "She'll be all right."

Sheena bent over her child, kneading and pushing as Kezia directed.

Then Kezia stood up, grey faced, took off her apron and laid it gently over Gudrun's head.

"Come, Sheena," she ordered quietly. "We'll get the wee lassie back to the house. I sent Jim to fetch the men."

Sheena was scarcely conscious of what went on thereafter: the astonished shouts of the men turning to anguish, the tramping of feet as Gudrun's body was carried into the house, the sobs, then the heavy, heavy stillness. Andy and Kezia rubbed warmth and life into Sheena's aching body.

"Helen," she whispered.

"She's asleep. She'll be fine," choked Andy.

Sheena could not say 'Gudrun' but she knew, and looked at Andy, wordlessly, her eyes huge in her strained, drawn face.

Big Mick and Jemmy were silent and uneasy, assiduously helping everybody with everything in every conceivable way – as though atoning for the guilt that lay ever more heavily now. Peter went out to walk on the shore – alone.

Old Kezia was with Gudrun, doing what had to be done; and washing, combing and arranging the golden hair to cover the great purple bruise on her brow.

Sheena slept at last – heavily – and awoke, dazed, and disbelieving what she remembered. Ignoring the others, she stumbled outside in the half dark, across the heather to where she and Gudrun had so idly and happily passed the afternoon. She picked up their knitting, now a discarded symbol of unfinished life. Gudrun's was a sweater for Peter. Sheena clutched it to her, breaking into wild weeping. "I'll finish it, I'll finish it," she sobbed.

Calming herself, she sat alone, trying to come to terms with what had happened. If Helen had not fallen, if wee Jim had not knocked the boulder down, if the men had not all been on the shore. There's a lot of things I'll have to try to finish for Gudrun, she thought grimly.

She went back to the house. The men sat heavy and silent, the children wide-eyed, pale and uncomprehending. Sheena looked at them and spoke steadily. "We all need something to eat and then we must think of the right place to put Gudrun," she said.

In the morning, Peter went out and found a place on the machair, within sight of the sea, among the wild flowers she so often painted. Andy carved a little wooden cross.

"What will I put on it?" he asked Peter.

"Put 'Princess Gudrun lies here'," whispered Helen.

"No, no, Love," muttered Andy.

"Yes," said Peter fiercely. "She'd like that; it would make her laugh. She was a princess in every way a child thinks of one. She was beautiful and kind. She never hurt anybody in all of her life."

Mick and Jemmy stared at the floor.

Helen picked the last of the year's flowers, and a bright branch of the rowan, and they put them on the narrow grave.

Kezia, her white hair and apron blowing in the salt-laden wind from the sea, read from her big black bible about green pastures.

"She will always be here with us," said Sheena. It was her only comment.

CHAPTER 11

I n the days and weeks that followed it was Sheena's steadfast determination that kept their depleted community living and working together as usual. Peter remained aloof, keeping his thoughts to himself. Mick and Jemmy passed him with averted eyes. Andy and Angus were heavy and silent as they worked at the boat. Even Kezia was weary and exhausted – death had visited her doorstep too often – but she watched Sheena's efforts with recognition and appreciation as Sheena worked, consoled, urged, coaxed and talked cheerfully to the children, trying to rekindle the laughter and enthusiasm that seemed to have died with Gudrun.

"Ay, Lass," said Kezia. "It's easier to repair the clothes than the minds and the bodies. We'll just have to keep putting one foot in front of the other till the edge of the grief is gone." She sighed heavily.

One morning Peter came to the McBrides' door, his rucksack on his back, and Gudrun's basket in his hand. Sheena and Andy looked in consternation. "I'm off for a bit," he said. "I need to get away, and folk here will recover more quickly without me around. I'd like to find a way of letting Gudrun's folk know. If I go to the east coast, there may be some boats going by now."

He looked at their concerned faces and smiled suddenly. "I will be back, you know," he said. "This was the place Gudrun and I chose together. It's a good place, and I know you will take care of everything."

"Oh, God!" thought Sheena, biting back the tears. "He's never said a word of blame to us."

She put a hand on his arm. "I'm that sorry," she faltered.

"I know," he said. "It's worse for you, but nobody meant it to happen. I've watched you the last weeks, and I know how much you are suffering. You know Gudrun wouldn't want that for any of us."

He turned to Helen. "Here," he urged. "Take these. Gudrun would like you to have them. She thought you could be good." He gave her the basket, full of paints, brushes and paper. "Mind you have plenty of pictures for me when I get back. Keep up the spelling and the tables... and you too, wee Jim."

"I'll see tae it," said Sheena firmly. Life with Gudrun and Kezia, the one with her books, the other with age-old wisdom and skills, had taught her what learning was all about. She wanted nothing better than that her children should acquire some of this knowledge.

CHAPTER 12

With Peter and Gudrun gone, the daily chores kept all of them busy. Andy and Angus had decided that Mick and Jemmy could get another house ready for themselves – to keep them busy over the winter. With Frank and Steve as willing, and now experienced helpers, they spent much time clearing and preparing.

After one of these sessions Frank came up to Andy. "That wee Sandy youse knew, him that gave youse the boots 'an all. Big Mick tells us he got put off his allotment."

Andy went to Mick and, for the first time since Mick's attack on Gudrun, had a long talk with him, piecing together all that had happened since their departure.

Sandy's allotment had been raided. He had woken up one morning to find his produce cleaned out, and even the fence taken for firewood. Forced back to the confines of his room in the tower block, old and tired, he had lost the will to fight on.

Margaret had evidently done her best to care for him. Her life had taken a turn for the worse too. Dougie had beaten her up once too often, just as Andy and Sheena had suspected, and been taken away by the police. They were all living a hand-to-mouth existence.

Andy was deeply troubled. He leaned against Mick's door and looked around the glen, and thought of Sandy's enthusiasm and wisdom that had brought him here in the first place. He couldn't bear to think of him shut in – cold and hungry.

By the time he reached home his decision was almost made, and over the evening fire, he talked it out with Sheena.

"I just feel I should go doon tae see to him. It's because o' him we're safe up here, and anyway, it would let us see whit's goin on since we left, if there's any word from the outside, and who is in charge. But I don't like leaving you and the bairns, now that Peter's away, and Gudrun…" He paused.

There was a time when Sheena would have been anxious and afraid, but that time had gone. "We'll manage fine," she said. "I have Angus and Kezia; and Frank and Steve are able for anything now. Mebbe you should take that Jemmy with you. He's more restless than Big Mick. I never know what to make of him."

So it was decided. Andy rechecked the house for wind and rain, looked to the turf stack and gave instructions to Big Mick, Frank and Steve. The first light fall of snow had come to the glen when they were ready to leave. Andy's rucksack was brought out and packed with the sleeping bag and a parcel of fresh soda scones and hard-boiled eggs, and a big jar of Kezia's honey to start them on their way. Sheena looked with pride at their warm woollen jerseys and balaclavas and gloves as they put them on – her summer's work.

"Well," said Andy, "we'll be no longer than we have to, but I dunno how long it will take."

"I know fine," said Sheena gamely, remembering the journey up, "but you're in better shape now, and ye'll no have us hinging on, nor the handcart." She gave him a bleak smile. "Don't forget to bring us pie and chips!"

"Bring me a Cindy doll, Daddy," called Helen.

"And what about wee Jim?" asked Andy, but Jim could think of nothing he needed.

They waved goodbye until they were out of sight, over the hump of the hill. Sheena blinked back the tears – Andy had never left her before.

"I've the kettle on for tea, Lass," said Kezia, with understanding.

Andy and Jemmy reached the top of the road by late afternoon. They were warm with walking, but could feel the piercing cold of the air around them. Andy noted the light flurries of snow, which were whitewashing the big peaks. They turned onto the main road, planning to light their fire and shelter for the night under the first bridge. But, in the first lay-by, they came upon a group of the peat men going down to Glasgow with laden carts. Their luck was in, and lifts were soon ensured. The evening passed jovially around a great roaring fire, with many a brew-up, and a dram or two to keep out the cold. The peat men were a great source of information, bringing news of other groups of survivors; what they were doing, or growing; and the possibilities of barter and exchange.

The morning found them rattling down the road at a fair old pace, Andy marvelling at the time it had taken them to travel up. He pointed out to the peat man, Jock McPhee, the landmarks of that epic journey: the head of the glen where the big house was, the place on the moor where they camped, starving. They stopped again at the inn of the great fires and the feet-tapping music, and Andy and Jemmy shared a vast old four-poster bed for the night.

Andy told the landlord about his new life in the glen and his present mission.

"Well, bring that Sandy here for the night on your way back," he invited. "I'd like fine to see him again." Andy was taken aback. He had not thought of bringing Sandy back. He wanted only to see how he was and what he could do for him, and what life was like since they left. He mused, absorbed in this new idea. Well – why not? The wee man would be a tonic to all with his stories and singing, and a great help with his wisdom and practical skills. He and old Angus would have a great crack together, and new faces were sorely needed to counter the loss and desolation Gudrun's death had brought to them.

Andy remained lost in thought as the peat cart rattled and bumped its way over the potholed roads, only lifting his head to look searchingly for the tinkers' camp, but Malachy had moved his brood on to fresh pastures.

As they came in to the outskirts of the city, his interest in his surroundings reawakened, and he began to look intently around him, with a sense of shock. He felt he was seeing the city, familiar to him for over thirty years, for the first time. The tower blocks were scabby and peeling. The skeleton shapes of the gantries were spectres of the prosperity of another generation. He looked at the peeling advertisements on the billboards: 'Glasgow is miles better'. A brave try.

Andy closed his eyes for a moment and thought of the bright freshness of the glen; of the white bay; of the little house, with space about it; of the work he looked forward to doing each day, and the satisfaction it gave him at the end of it. He had never been a great thinker, but over the months Peter and Gudrun's arguments about the rights and wrongs of things, and Angus's and Kezia's

age-old wisdom and innate kindness had had an effect on him.
He had learned to weigh up and compare and look with an aware,
critical eye. Before the journey north he had never been in charge
of his own destiny, always the dumb recipient of others' organisa-
tion – dole money, doctor's prescription, bingo cards, the pools,
HP. He had accepted them all without question; led his life on
scraps of paper, endlessly at other people's disposal.

His reverie was interrupted by Jemmy – voluble for once –
chattering excitedly as he pointed to familiar landmarks.

The city closed around them as they went like flies into its
great spider's web of dark street tunnels. Jock put them down
hurriedly at the top of Buchanan Street. Jemmy disappeared
eagerly in search of familiar acquaintances and old haunts. Andy
wondered if he would ever see him again.

Jock called back from the cart, "I'll be going back in two
days. If you are ready then, you can find me up at the hospital."
He clattered rapidly off, not wishing to risk his load at the hands of
looters. Andy walked slowly down the once-fashionable shopping
street. The great shops stared blankly; their glassless windows
empty plundered caves.

It was almost dark when he reached his old home. He remembered the cheery crowd and gala atmosphere of the day they left,
but now all was silent, cold, and desolate as an uncared-for grave-
yard. Then he noticed, in a corner made by two walls, a small
fire was struggling – more grey smoke than flame. So there was
some sign of life. He turned into his building, groped his way up
the stone stair and stood on the threshold of his erstwhile home.
He instinctively reached for the light switch and then laughed
wryly at himself. There was an all-pervading smell of damp and
decay. There was little he could do about Sandy till the morning,

Andy reflected. It was going to be a cold night. He'd better get a pot down to the fire, and brew up some tea, and then maybe see who was still around in the tower block. There was not a sound from the flat opposite. He went down to the fire, his steps echoing noisily in the funnel of the staircase. It was almost out. He kicked it into further efforts with his boots, and put the pot on. Out of the darkness a small figure approached, dragging an old pram. Recognition on both sides was sudden and shocked.

"Andy," said Margaret's voice. "Whit are ye deyin' here? Have ye come back? Where's Sheena and the bairns?"

Andy put an arm around her shoulders, appalled at her emaciated face and black shadowed eyes – haggard even in the firelight. "Are ye all right, Lass?" He faltered. "I heard the new baby had arrived. Big Mick told me."

"Och, Andy," said Margaret wearily, "then ye know about Dougie, and whit happened. I'm better off without him. It wis never much o' a marriage anyway, but with things as they are, I don't know where to turn next. If it wasn't for Sandy, we'd be dead."

"Sandy?" said Andy sharply.

"He's wi' me," said Margaret. "When the allotment was wrecked, he'd no place to stay, and when the polis took Dougie away I was right glad of his company. He looked after wee Beth when the baby came. Mrs Mulloy helped me too, but they're away noo, doon to the coast. There's a lot campin' there somewhere, waitin' to get over to Ireland. Sandy's no very well the noo." She looked anxiously at Andy.

"Well, wee'll soon see what's what," said Andy, as cheerfully as he could muster. He inspected the pathetic scraps of wood in the pram and wished he'd thought to bring a sack of turf from the cart. "Here, Hen," he said, "we'll put the lot on, and get a good blaze and boil the water up quick, and then we'll get back up, and see what we can sort for Sandy."

Andy went fast up the stairs. Margaret trailed apathetically behind, coming forward to help him shove open the door, which stuck – warped and misshapen with the damp.

A guttering candle showed the indescribable squalor of the room. On a mattress in a corner lay Sandy, evidently asleep and breathing heavily; and little Beth, asleep too, her cheeks hollow, and hands on the quilt, like little claws. Andy peered into the cot, where the baby snuffled. The smell was overpowering. Wet washing hung on chairs, dirty pots lay on the table. There was a stench of urine and rot.

"I've been that tired," said Margaret defensively.

"It's all right, Lass," said Andy gently. Up and down those stairs endlessly, with a baby and a toddler and an old man to care for – she's got guts to have stuck it, he thought, then reflected that she hadn't had much choice.

He wondered what to do next. Sheena would have known better in this set-up. It had been a long day and he felt exhausted.

"Don't wake Sandy noo," he whispered to Margaret. "I'll go back to my own place and tomorrow we'll think what's best to be done."

Despite his tiredness, he slept poorly, turning and tossing and eventually getting up in the chill, grey dawn to shiver down to the fire for a thankful cup of tea.

Before he opened Margaret's door, he could hear Sandy coughing. The old man had raised himself and lay propped against the wall, but both arms were outstretched eagerly to greet him.

"Andy, lad! It's great tae see you. Hoo's it going up there?"

Typically, not a word about his own plight. Andy could hear the wheeze in his chest, and see how he gasped for breath.

"I'll tell ye all aboot it," said Andy, "but first we're going to have our breakfast."

He still had a bit of Kezia's soda bread left, though somewhat stale, and the big pot of honey. He divided it among them and spread it liberally, Beth's great hungry eyes following his every movement.

"That'll be the real McKay – the heather honey," said Sandy, eating with relish.

"Ay, it is that," confirmed Andy with a sigh, seeing in his mind's eye the hives in the heather on the glenside, with the wild roses and the honeysuckle tumbling over the stone wall behind.

He began to tell them all about the glen – Kezia and Angus, Peter and Gudrun and what had happened to them. The peat cutting, his house, Helen's painting, Jim's fishing, the furniture making, the boat – all came tumbling out, making magic by bringing light and laughter and sunshine into the squalor and the drab room, and animation and interest to the worn, listless faces of its occupants.

Sandy lay back with eyes closed, drinking it all in, a look of deep pleasure on his face. When all was told, there was a little silence.

"It must be great up there," said Margaret timidly.

Andy's heart went out to them. He stood up. "I didnae tell you why I came back," he said, firmly and untruthfully. "I came to take yis all back with me."

A flicker of delight, then followed by a look of distress, came to Margaret's face.

"But the wee ones – I could nae."

"Och, we'll manage," declared Andy.

Two great tears sped down Sandy's cheeks.

"I'm too old and feeble – I'd haud ye back. I'm glad for Margaret; it'll gie them a chance. You're a guid man, Andy, to think of it."

"I'm not budging oot o' here without you," said Andy stoutly. "I'm away to make the arrangements. You start packing, Margaret. Only necessities, mind." Not that there was much else in the room anyway.

When he left the block, he scolded himself fiercely. "Oh, ye great loon. Whit have ye got yersel into noo? Two babies and a half-dead old man, and that Margaret nothing but skin and bone, and snow on the ground too." But he knew he could not leave them there. They would die, and he could not live with that realisation. Like Margaret, he had no choice.

He went out with no clear plan. If Jemmy was coming back it would help; and if the peat man, Jock, could be persuaded to bring the cart for Sandy and Margaret, he and Jemmy could walk and somehow get them down to the glen between them. It was a worrying thought, for it was December now. Soon be Christmas, he remembered, though not much sign of it around here. He set off to look for Jemmy. His search took him through the Barras. A few stallholders huddled miserably over their dwindling stock. People were not interested in anything they could not eat or burn. Something clicked in Andy's mind, and he turned back to a stall hanging with overstuffed toys, dolls with fluorescent hair, and garishly coloured animals, obscenely bright in their dismal surroundings.

"Have ye a Cindy doll?" he enquired.

"I could gie ye six dozen," sighed the stallholder.

"One'll dey the noo," grinned Andy.

He bought a lego set for Jim, an apron for Kezia, a tablecloth and cushion covers for Sheena, and felt his fast-diminishing money was well spent. Then he trudged up to the hospital, told his tale to Jock, and the decent man agreed to pick them up if they could be ready first thing in the morning. His remaining money was spent on two tins of beans, given reluctantly and handed through a grille, at a wee shop where he was known. With these he fed his little group of cast-offs, whose future now lay in his hands.

In the evening, pleased enough with the way his arrangements were taking shape, he went out again to look for Jemmy, going from one street fire to another – the only sign of community life left. In the end Jemmy found him, calling from a dark alleyway, where he was seated, hunched up on a bin. Although Jemmy was habitually a man of few words and inclined to be morose, Andy sensed something was wrong.

"What's up?" he enquired.

"Ye ken Noddy?"

"Aye," said Andy, remembering Noddy trotting along, pulling the cart and whooping through the road, dragging out branches.

"Whit aboot him?"

"Well, he's deid," sniffed Jemmy.

"The glue?" queried Andy.

"Aye. Likely that was it."

"That's bloody," said Andy.

Jemmy and Noddy had been close: two derelicts of their times, fathers in and out of Barlinnie, mothers downtrodden and ineffective, wee hard men from when they were able to walk, mitching school, petty crime, in and out of children's homes, remand homes, assessment centres – products of state 'care'.

Their common background had formed an inarticulate bond between them.

"Well, Lad, I'm sorry," Andy said awkwardly. "What are ye going to do? Do you want to come back up with me?"

"Oh aye," said Jemmy. "Naethin' to dey here any more. It's guid up there anyway."

Andy was surprised. Jemmy had never shown any enthusiasm for life in the glen, but then his arrival had been under a cloud, and he was never one to express his emotions anyway, following Big Mick like a silent shadow.

Andy told him about Sandy and Margaret. Jemmy was aghast. "But ye cannie get them up there; it was snowin' on the way doon. Two bairns and ould Sandy. Ach, yer saft in the heid."

"Well, I'm no leaving them to starve, that's for sure," growled Andy. He did not need Jemmy to confirm what he already felt. "If you're coming, be round at the hoose for nine in the morning."

"OK, OK," muttered Jemmy, kicking at the bin.

CHAPTER 13

The clatter of hooves in the distance announced the arrival of the cart to the pathetic little group who waited in the chill air. Sandy, bundled up in his anorak and wee red bobble hat, sat on a chair with a rug wrapped round him. Margaret had wrapped a blanket-like shawl about herself and the baby. Andy held Beth – light as a leaf. Their meagre belongings were at their feet, shoved into black, plastic bin bags. Jemmy lurched round the corner in time to help Andy and Jock with the loading. They lined the cart with rugs and pillows from the beds to try to ease the jolting, and they covered them with the tarpaulin. Jock's plan was to make for one of his usual camping spots along the loch shore for the night, and Andy and Jemmy hoped to get a lift in another cart, in time to join them.

Andy's relief as he watched them off was tinged with worry at the thought of the journey ahead of them. He picked up his rucksack, and gazed up for a moment at his old home. It was meaningless to him now – that jumble of furniture in that grey little concrete box, away up there. That was no way to live – like battery hens, all stashed away, and your front door opening to a lift shaft instead of green grass and fresh air.

He left without a backward glance, setting a great pace. Jemmy, puffing to keep up, said suddenly, "I'n't it good to be goin' home." Andy was astonished and gratified.

A couple of hours later, and they could see the hills, plastered white, but the sky was blue. On the edge of the city Jock's friend Fergus picked them up. He'd heard from Jock in the morning what was going on, and had been looking out for them. The loch shore was breathtaking in the sunshine. All was a-dazzle and a-glitter, half blinding them in its brilliance of blue and white. The conifers were heavy with snow, and on the bare branches of the bushes little frozen ice drops glittered and tinkled. The road became white and crunchy.

Soon they saw Jock's cart in the distance. The little red bobble hat was clearly visible, turning this way and that.

Andy chuckled. "Sandy's getting a good day. There's life in him yet. Look at the way he's taking it all in!"

Sandy was indeed ecstatic when they reached him. His face was pink with cold and excitement.

"Man, Andy, I never thought I'd be back here. This is great," he crowed. "If I died te day, I'd die happy!"

"Ah, put yer heid doon and keep warm," laughed Andy, pulling the blankets closely around him. Margaret and her babies seemed to be asleep.

They made good time and unexpectedly reached the old hostelry before dark. The innkeeper and his son carried Sandy to a seat in front of the fire, where great blazing logs were exploding sparks into the dark chimney. Margaret's family were soon made comfortable, and Andy and Jemmy spent the evening, warm and half-asleep, listening to Sandy – in his element reminiscing with the landlord about the characters of the cycling clubs and the mountaineering clubs, and the exploits of the lads of the old Craigdhu. The wee man seemed to have taken on a new lease of life.

In the morning the innkeeper shook Andy awake. "It's bad news I have to bring you," he said. "I went to take him in a cup of tea. I have to tell you that our good old friend died in the night."

"Whit?" said Andy, at first drowsy and uncomprehending, then stunned and incredulous.

"But he was fine last night. Och, I shouldna have brought him. It was too much for him. He wasna well enough."

The innkeeper interrupted Andy's self-reproach.

"He died in his sleep, and he died happy. From what you told me, that wouldn't have been the case if you'd left him behind. From what I know of him that's the way he'd have wanted to go. Yesterday he had the chance to relive all the bits of his life that mattered to him. What more can a man want before he dies?" he ventured. "I've discussed it with my son before I came to tell you. We'll bury him here, in sight of the loch and the Ben. He'd like that."

There was no time to mourn Sandy, nor for the diminished little group to attend his funeral, for the sky was laden and ominous and the turf men anxious to be gone. They had to make haste while they could, and in any case the innkeeper did not have provisions to feed extra mouths for long. They had a dish of porridge, and before they left the innkeeper handed over to Andy Sandy's watch and wallet – all his savings.

"Had he any relatives?"

"None that I know of," said Andy.

By the afternoon, they were on the moor, in howling wind and driving snow. The little convoy of carts kept close together, the men trudging alongside, urging the horses on, and digging and pushing for each other when the going was hard. Margaret and the children stayed tucked up, with hot-water bottles and blankets, under the tarpaulin. That night, they spent shivering round a fire in an old barn. The next afternoon saw them through Fort William in ever-deepening snow. Two more days of struggle, and trudging and pushing, and they were at the head of the glen road.

"This is where I have to leave you," said Jock, uneasily and apologetically. Andy understood. Jock would have a hard struggle to win home himself. The cart's wheels were sticking at every turn and it might have to be abandoned.

"Leave the bags on the cart," said Jock. "I'll get them to you sometime. Good luck."

All the familiar landmarks, except the high peaks, were blotted out in the great white snow blanket. Even the noisy burn was silenced by the icy fingers which gripped it. Andy's heart sank – he and Jemmy would have a job to get through on their own, never mind with the frail Margaret and the children. Jemmy put Beth, wailing in the sudden exposure to the cold – on his shoulders. Andy put his rucksack on his back, and the baby inside his warm anorak.

Fortunately, wee Hope was too small to realise, or feel anything except hunger, and so far Margaret had managed to keep her fed. The two men would go on in front, and tramp a path, and Margaret would just have to follow as best she could. Thus they made their way for some considerable time, until the first flakes flickering on their cheeks indicated another snowfall.

Andy swore. He had hoped to get further down, to where there was an old bothy where they could shelter and rest. Beth, unaccustomed to such exposure, would freeze, perched up on

Jemmy's shoulders like that, and Margaret could scarcely drag herself along. Panic arose within him. He forced it aside.

"We're no goin' to give in ten miles from home," he declared firmly. Dragging the sleeping bag from his loaded rucksack, he wrapped it round Beth, and urged Jemmy on. He held out an arm to Margaret as she floundered, knee deep in the soft snow. Clinging together, they fought on, clambering in and out of drifts, stumbling over buried logs, caught up at times in the prickly conifers. The flakes fell on their defenceless faces, like blobs of wet cotton wool. The seemingly gentle feathers searched out every crevice in their clothing, melting into icy trickles on their cringing skin. Never even sure if they were on the road, Andy saw at last, through the whirling snowflakes, the outline of the bothy. A few kicks and shoves, and they had the door open. Margaret fell to the ground, half senseless, and Andy and Jemmy knelt, rubbing her feet and hands and face, white as the snow itself.

"God! Are we going to lose her too?" gasped Andy.

"I'll get a fire going," said Jemmy. "There's plenty branches lying about back there, and I can break up those old tattie boxes."

"Wee'll have to stay here for the night," said Andy. "Margaret's no fit to go on."

They fed the baby and Beth, and put Margaret in the sleeping bag next the warming fire. It was still early afternoon, and it was going to be a long night. Andy lay back on the old straw which covered the floor, aching in every limb.

Jemmy looked at him. "Yer eyes are bloodshot," he announced, then, after a moment's consideration, "I'll go on ahead and tell them we're here. Mick can come and help us."

Andy started. Ten miles by himself in the snow – could the lad manage it? He forced his weary mind to weigh up the situation. He thought of Big Mick's great strength; they could use it tomorrow. There might not be enough wood to see them through the night. What a fool he'd been to take such risks. Then his mind strayed again to the squalid flat in the tower block. He tried to concentrate.

"Well, go on, Jemmy, lad," he said wearily. "Mind how you go, and all the best."

"See you," said Jemmy, and he was off.

Andy dozed, worn out, when he was gone, and was awakened suddenly by howls of hunger from the baby. Margaret woke too, and sat up. It was dark and the fire had gone down.

"Andy," said Margaret, "Where are we?"

He told her. She seemed to have walked the last miles without seeing or feeling anything. She got up, holding on to the wall, and saw to the baby.

She's got guts, thought Andy again.

The hours passed, and they waited numbly for morning, dozing a little, putting a few more pieces on the fire, trying to conserve the small stock of wood for as long as possible. The baby wailed intermittently, and Beth stirred and moaned in her sleep. Andy, never a religious man, prayed inwardly, incoherently.

Then suddenly there came a muffled shout from the dark night outside. Andy leapt to his feet, aches and pains forgotten. Could it be?

"We're here, we're here," he bawled, hurling open the door. A second later, Big Mick's great frame hove into sight, a hurricane lantern in his fist. Behind him were Frank and Steve. Both were laden. From their sacks came a tin, and a bottle of soup to be heated in it; oats; cakes and cheese; soda bread; and a bag of peat. Sheena and Kezia had thought and packed well.

"How's Jemmy?" said Andy, when the excitement and delight of greeting had abated. How that lad must have moved!

"He's half deid," said Mick, "but he's OK."

He looked curiously at Margaret, who was revived and smiling now, the firelight dancing in her green eyes and lighting up her red-brown hair. Mick winked at her.

Andy was momentarily amused. Margaret could take care of herself – less gently reared than Gudrun – but for the moment he had more passing things to consider. Too tired to talk further, he keeled over, and slept, motionless and soundly.

It was a transformed little party which set off next morning. The young ones bounced along, throwing snowballs and swinging little Beth between them. Big Mick was everywhere, showing off his great strength, laden with everyone's baggage, kicking and bashing a path for all, helping Margaret carefully and considerately through the snowdrifts. Andy would trust little Hope to no one but himself. As they topped the brow of the hill and looked down, they could see figures below watching, and then running about and waving energetically.

Then they all came running – Helen and wee Jim out in front, Sheena and Jemmy, Kezia following – to surround them with delight and affection. Andy hugged his family as if he would never see them again. They seemed so sturdy and rosy-cheeked and sweet-smelling. He looked with renewed concern at the stick-like Margaret, and her half-starved children. Kezia took the baby from him.

"What's her name?" she smiled at Margaret.

"Hope," said Margaret. "It was ma gran's name. It's a bit old-fashioned."

"No," said Kezia, looking into the distance. "Hope is never old-fashioned."

Sheena soon had Margaret into the comfort of the school-house, and the children bathed and fed.

At last Andy and Sheena had a minute alone before the red peat fire in their own home. As Andy told her all that had happened, his pent-up feelings were released, and great sobs shook him as he relived the last day with Sandy. Sheena cried too, and they both consoled each other, until Helen, bursting in from helping in the schoolhouse, cried in distress, "Daddy, Daddy, Mammy. Why are you crying? It's Christmas!"

"Christmas?" said Andy, dazed.

"Aye," said Sheena. "Och, ye've lost track of the time, and no wonder. It's Christmas Day!"

"And Kezia's killed the big goose, and we're all going to eat it," chatted Helen, "and I decorated the Christmas tree at the schoolhouse, and I painted stars for it, and Frank and Steve made wee birds out of wood."

"And I," said Andy, with a great laugh, "am Santa Claus."

From the bottom of his rucksack he brought out his presents. It seemed years ago, in another world, since he had bought them.

In the evening, rested and renewed, they all went to the schoolhouse and ate the great goose, and tatties and turnips. They drank Angus's elderberry wine, and joked and laughed and sang in the lamplight around the warm fire.

"I'll never forget this Christmas," said Sheena sleepily.

Andy was deeply content. He had brought some new life into the glen. The children would have their chance to be healthy and happy, and would be a focus of interest for the adults around them. With Sandy's money they could buy a cow for milk for the children. His own were not too keen on the goat's. Maybe a horse too, to replace the tottering Neddy, now only fit for donkey rides. It would be good to have some form of transport in an emergency.

So, planning happily, he slept – quickly and soundly.

CHAPTER 14

The winter passed, bringing good days and bad. Days when the wind bashed in from the sea, driving the rain before it, turning the ground into sticky sludge underfoot, lashing the house with its salty tongue. Then the glen was no Garden of Eden, but it was still far better than anything they had known before, and there was work to keep them busy in the houses, and company to do it with.

On one morning, when the frosts had finally vanished for another year, and the sky was cloudless, and the sea calm, sparkling and dazzling in the sun, Andy rowed slowly across the bay to set a few lobster pots on the rocks off the little island. He rowed cautiously at first, clumsily, oars slipping and splashing, then with increasing confidence as the boat surged forward despite his ineptitude. He persisted, his face burning in the sun, his arm muscles screaming, until at last the keel grated on the coarse sand of the little island beach. He threw himself on the soft turf of the machair for a well-earned rest, and stared about him with a dawning awareness of the beauty of it all. He looked at the sea pinks against the grey rocks, the white shell-strewn sand, the little weedy pools, and, beyond, the blinding sparkle of the sea. The outer rocks were jammed with seals – big black ones and little grey-and-white ones, all huffing and puffing and grunting and humping themselves in and out of the water. He'd have to bring the young ones out to see them. He drew a breath of pure exultation, and lay back with closed eyes, listening to the soft, undulating cooing of the eider ducks as they marshalled their little flotillas around the rocky bays.

Gradually he became aware of a different sound, louder, increasingly louder – a steady drone.

He sat up, then stood up, staring in disbelief. It was an aeroplane. Andy cheered and shouted, waving his arms and rushing about on the shingle, until it disappeared – a minute speck in the distance. So the shutdown was over. Someone, somewhere, had found a solution.

Then, slowly, he sat down. What would it mean? Would everything be as before? What about his family, the glen, and the people in it? Before, there had been no worthwhile choice. Now, they would all have to choose what to do next. His first elation was replaced by a feeling of apprehension. Sheena? What would she want? He pushed the boat out with a heavy heart, staring towards the glen and the children playing on the beach.

Sheena was in the house when he got back, and had obviously not heard the plane. He told her the news, watching her face. It was expressionless.

She walked slowly and deliberately to the door and stood looking out, thinking hard. Phrases of Gudrun's came drifting back: "Ordinary people got left out", "…became almost machines themselves", "…all the old skills lost". She felt she understood them better now.

She turned and looked at Andy's worried face.

"Well," she said, "that's guid news. Now maybe we can get a wee car or van. It will help you in the boatyard you're always talking about starting up, and maybe we'll get the odd jaunt to Fort William."

Andy laughed aloud. A great load fell from him. He hugged Sheena, and together they went out to talk to the others. Whatever happened now, there was interest and promise, and hope for tomorrow.